P9-BAU-285

Praise for THE ROMAN MYSTERIES

'From slave traders to criminal masterminds, Flavia Gemina and her fellow sleuths outwit a host of villains in these riveting Roman detective stories. No one is writing crime for children like Caroline Lawrence' *Waterstones*

'Packed with adventure and effortlessly deployed detail culled from Pliny and Juvenal . . . enjoyable entertainment' *The Independent on Sunday*

'. . . a fresh type of historical novel full of drama and fun . . . This series promises many delights to come' *The Times*

'Lively characters, exciting plotlines and the vivid evocation of life in Ancient Rome makes this series hugely popular' *Borders Summer Magazine*

'Lawrence has succeeded in not only vividly and accurately recreating the world of ancient Rome, but has also written some really exciting, child-centred thriller stories . . .' *Northern Echo*

'A great read for kids' *Daily Express*

Also by Caroline Lawrence

THE ROMAN MYSTERIES

Trimalchio's Feast and Other Mini-Mysteries
The Legionary from Londinium and Other Mini-Mysteries

THE ROMAN MYSTERY SCROLLS

THE P.K. PINKERTON MYSTERIES

The ROMAN MYSTERIES

BOOK I

The Thieves of Ostia

CAROLINE LAWRENCE

Orion
Children's Books

ORION CHILDREN'S BOOKS

First published in Great Britain in 2001 by Orion Children's Books
Paperback edition first published in 2002 by Dolphin Paperbacks
Reissued in 2012 by Orion Children's Books
This edition published in 2016 by Hodder and Stoughton

41

Copyright © Roman Mysteries Ltd, 2001
Maps by Richard Russell Lawrence © Orion Children's Books, 2001

The moral rights of the author and illustrator have been asserted.

*All characters and events in this publication, other than those clearly
in the public domain, are fictitious and any resemblance to
real persons, living or dead, is purely coincidental.*

All rights reserved.
No part of this publication may be reproduced, stored in
a retrieval system, or transmitted, in any form or by any means, without
the prior permission in writing of the publisher, nor be otherwise circulated
in any form of binding or cover other than that in which it is published
and without a similar condition including this condition being
imposed on the subsequent purchaser.

A CIP catalogue record for this book
is available from the British Library.

ISBN 978 1 84255 020 5

Printed and bound in Great Britain by
Clays Ltd, Elcograf S.p.A.

The paper and board used in this book are
made from wood from responsible sources.

MIX
Paper from
responsible sources
FSC® C104740

Orion Children's Books
An imprint of
Hachette Children's Group
Part of Hodder & Stoughton
Carmelite House
50 Victoria Embankment
London EC4Y 0DZ

An Hachette UK Company
www.hachette.co.uk

www.hachettechildrens.co.uk
www.romanmysteries.com

To my mother and father,
for all their love and support

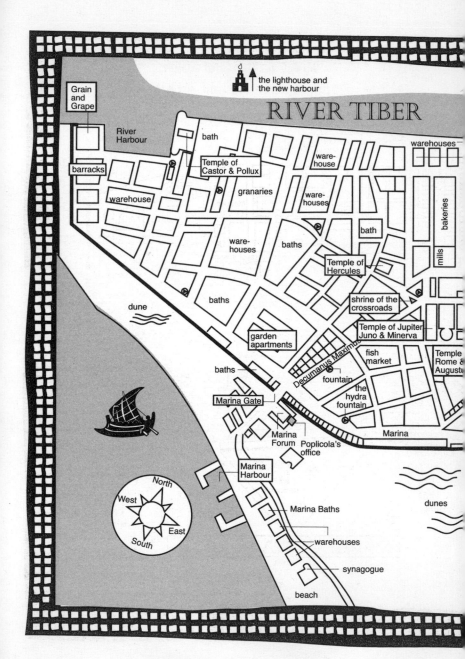

the lighthouse and
the new harbour

RIVER TIBER

Grain
and
Grape

River
Harbour

warehouses

barracks

bath

warehouse

warehouses

Temple of
Castor & Pollux

granaries

warehouse

warehouses

bath

bakeries

mills

warehouse

baths

Temple of
Hercules

dune

baths

shrine of the
crossroads

Temple of Jupiter
Juno & Minerva

garden
apartments

fish
market

Temple of
Rome &
August[...]

Decumanus Maxim[...]

fountain

baths

the
hydra
fountain

Marina Gate

Marina

Marina
Forum

Poplicola's
office

North

West

Marina
Harbour

East

Marina Baths

South

dunes

warehouses

synagogue

beach

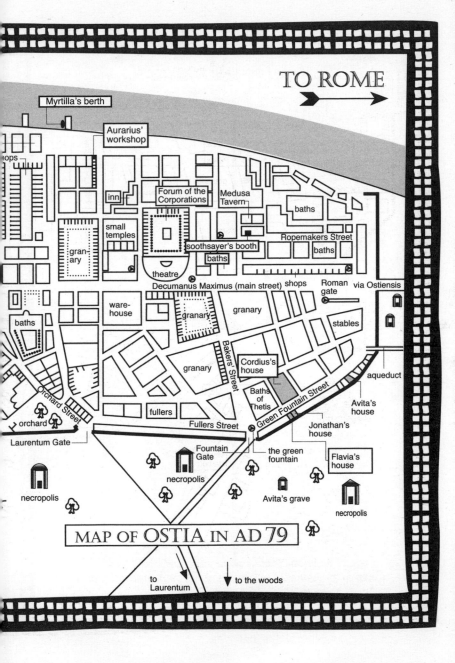

TO ROME

Myrtilla's berth

Aurarius' workshop

shops

inn

Forum of the Corporations

Medusa Tavern

baths

small temples

soothsayer's booth

Ropemakers Street

gran-ary

baths

baths

theatre

Decumanus Maximus (main street)

shops

Roman gate

via Ostiensis

ware-house

granary

granary

stables

baths

granary

Bakers' Street

Cordius's house

aqueduct

Orchard Street

granary

fullers

Baths of Thetis

Green Fountain Street

Avita's house

orchard

Fullers Street

Jonathan's house

Laurentum Gate

Fountain Gate

the green fountain

Flavia's house

necropolis

necropolis

Avita's grave

necropolis

MAP OF OSTIA IN AD 79

to Laurentum

to the woods

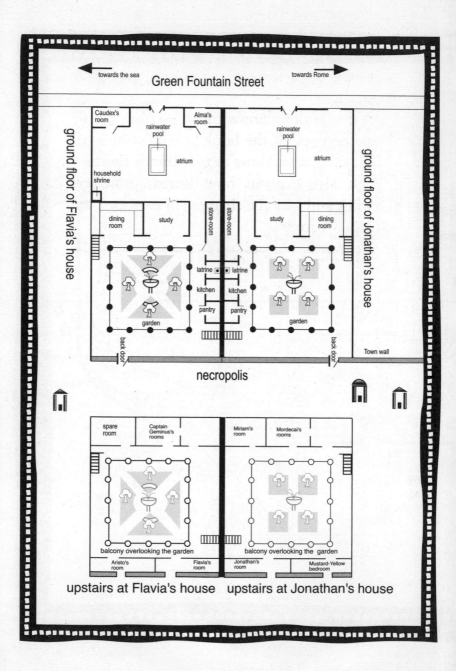

towards the sea ← Green Fountain Street → towards Rome

ground floor of Flavia's house

Caudex's room
rainwater pool
atrium
Alma's room
rainwater pool
atrium

household shrine

dining room
study
store-room
store-room
study
dining room

latrine • • latrine

kitchen
kitchen

pantry
pantry

garden
garden

back door
back door
Town wall

ground floor of Jonathan's house

necropolis

spare room
Captain Geminus's rooms
Miriam's room
Mordecai's rooms

balcony overlooking the garden
balcony overlooking the garden

Aristo's room
Flavia's room
Jonathan's room
Mustard-Yellow bedroom

upstairs at Flavia's house   upstairs at Jonathan's house

This story takes place in Ancient Roman times, so a few of the words may look strange.

If you don't know them, 'Aristo's Scroll' at the back of the book will tell you what they mean and how to pronounce them.

It also explains how Roman numbers work and why the chapters in this book are called 'scrolls'.

SCROLL I

Flavia Gemina solved her first mystery on the Ides of June in the tenth year of the Emperor Vespasian.

She had always had a knack for finding things her father misplaced: his best toga, his quill pen, and once even his ceremonial dagger. But this time there had been a real crime, with a real culprit.

It was a hot, still afternoon, for the sea breeze had not yet risen. Flavia had just settled herself in the garden by the fountain, with a cup of peach juice and her favourite scroll.

'Flavia? Flavia!' Her father's voice came from the study. Flavia took a sip of juice and quickly scanned the scroll to find her place. She would just read one or two lines. After all, the study was so close, just the other side of the fig tree. Her house – like many others in the Roman port of Ostia – had a secret garden at its centre, invisible to anyone on the street. From that inner garden it was only a few steps to the dining room, the kitchen, the store-room, a small latrine, and the study.

'Flavia!'

She knew that tone of voice.

'Coming, pater!' she called. Hastily, she set down her cup on the marble bench and placed a pebble on the open scroll to mark her place.

In the study, her father was desperately searching through various scrolls and sheets of parchment on the cedarwood table. Although Marcus Flavius Geminus was extremely competent aboard his own ship, on land he was hopelessly absent-minded.

'Oh pater!' Flavia tried to keep the impatience out of her voice. 'What have you lost now?'

'It isn't lost! It's been stolen!'

'What? What's been stolen?'

'My seal! My amethyst signet-ring! The one your mother gave me!'

'Oh!' She winced. Her mother had died in child-birth several years previously, and they both still missed her desperately.

Flavia touched her father's arm reassuringly. 'Don't worry, pater. I always find things, don't I?'

'Yes. Yes, you do . . .' He smiled down at her, but Flavia could see he was upset.

'Where did you last see it?' she asked.

'Right here on my desk. I was just letting these documents dry before I sealed them.'

Flavia's father planned to sail for Corinth at the end of the week. As a ship owner and captain, it was his responsibility to make sure the paperwork was ready.

'I left the study for just a moment to use the

latrine,' he explained. 'When I returned, the ring was gone. Look: the documents are here. The wax is here. The candle is here, still lit. But my ring is gone!'

'It wasn't the wind, there's no hint of a breeze,' Flavia mused, gazing out at the fig tree. 'The slaves are napping in their rooms. Scuto is sleeping under the jasmine bush: he didn't even bark. Yes, it's a mystery.'

'It's one of the few things of hers I have left,' murmured her father. 'And apart from that, I need it to seal these documents.' He ran a hand distractedly through his hair.

Flavia had an idea: 'Pater, do you have another seal?'

'Yes, but I rarely use it. My suppliers might not recognise it . . .'

'But it has Castor and Pollux engraved on it, doesn't it?'

Her father nodded. Castor and Pollux, the mythological twins known as the Gemini, had always been linked to the Geminus family.

'Well then, everyone will know it's yours. Why don't you use that ring to finish sealing the documents, and I'll try to find the stolen one.'

Captain Geminus's face relaxed and he looked at his daughter fondly.

'Thank you, my little owl.' He kissed the top of her head. 'What would I do without you?'

As her father went upstairs to search the chest in his bedroom, Flavia looked around. The study was a small, bright room with red and yellow plaster walls and a cool, marble floor. It was simply furnished with a cedarwood chair, the table which served as a desk, and a bronze standing-lamp. There was also a bust of the Emperor Vespasian on a pink marble column beside the desk.

The study had two doors. One small folding door led into the atrium at the front of the house. On the opposite wall a wide doorway opened directly out onto the inner garden. This could be closed off with a heavy curtain.

Now this curtain was pulled right back, and sunlight from the garden fell directly onto the desk, lighting up the sheets of parchment so that they seemed to glow. A little inkpot blazed silver in the sunshine. It was fixed onto the desk so that it would not go missing. For the same reason, the silver quill pen was attached to the desk by a silver chain. Flavia rolled the chain absently between her thumb and forefinger and observed how it flashed in the direct sunlight.

Suddenly her keen grey eyes noticed something. On one of the sheets of parchment – a list of ships' provisions – was a faint black mark that was neither a letter nor a number. Without touching anything, Flavia moved her face closer, until her nose was inches from the sheet.

No doubt about it. Someone – or something – had touched the ink while it was still tacky and had made this strange V-shaped mark. As she looked closer, Flavia could make out a straight line between the two leaning lines of the V, like the Greek letter *psi*: Ψ

At that moment, something rustled and flapped in the garden. Flavia glanced up and saw a large black and white bird sitting on a branch of the fig tree: a magpie. The bird turned its head and regarded her with one bright, intelligent eye.

In an instant, Flavia knew she was looking at the thief. She knew magpies loved glittering things. The bird had obviously stepped on the parchment before the ink had dried and then left its footprint.

Now she must discover where its nest was.

Flavia thought quickly. She needed bait; something bright and shiny. Without turning her head or making a sudden movement she surveyed the study. There were various scrolls stored on shelves along the walls, but they were parchment or papyrus, and their dangling labels only leather. The wax tablets on the desk were too big for the bird to carry and the little bronze oil-lamp too heavy.

There was only one thing she could think of to tempt the bird. Slowly she reached up to her throat and undid the clasp of a silver chain. Like every freeborn Roman boy or girl, Flavia wore a special amulet around her neck. One day, when she married, she would dedicate this bulla to the gods of the crossroads.

But for now, the chain it hung on would serve another useful purpose. Slipping the bulla into the coin purse which hung from her belt, she carefully set the chain in a pool of sunlight. It sparkled temptingly.

Slowly, Flavia backed out of the study and squeezed past the folding door into the cool, dim atrium. As soon as she was out of the magpie's sight, she crept along the short corridor which led back to the garden.

Peeping round the corner, she was just in time to see the magpie fly down into the study. Flavia held her breath and prayed her father would not come back and disturb the bird.

A moment later the magpie flew back up onto a branch, the chain dangling from its beak like a glittering worm. It remained there for a moment looking around, then flew away over the red-tiled roof to the south, towards the graveyard.

Flavia ran through the garden and opened the small back door. For an instant she hesitated.

She knew the heavy bolt would fall back into place behind her and she would be locked out. If she went through the doorway she would leave the protection not only of her home, but of Ostia: her house was built into the town wall.

Furthermore, the door led directly into the

necropolis, the 'city of the dead', with its many tombs and graves scattered among the trees, and her father had warned her never to go there.

But she had promised to find his ring: the ring her mother had given him.

Flavia took a deep breath and stepped out. The door shut behind her and she heard the bolt fall. There was no going back now.

She was just in time to glimpse a flutter of glossy black and white as the bird flew to a tall umbrella pine. She ran quickly and quietly, keeping the trunk of a large cypress tree between herself and the feathered thief.

The magpie flew off again and Flavia ran to the pine tree. Peeping out from behind it, she saw nothing; no movement anywhere. Her heart sank.

Then she saw it. In an old oak near a large tomb something flashed. Something flashed black and white. It was the magpie. It had popped up from the trunk of the oak like a cork ball in a pond, and its beak was empty!

For a few minutes the magpie preened itself smugly, no doubt pleased at its afternoon's haul. Presently it hopped onto a higher branch, cocked its head for a moment and flew back towards the north, probably to see if there was any treasure left in her house.

Flavia dodged among the tombs and trees and reached the old oak in no time. The bark was rough

7

and scratched her hands but its roughness helped her to get a good grip. She went up it with little difficulty.

When she reached the place where the trunk forked into branches, her eyes opened in amazement: a small treasure trove of bright objects glittered there. Her chain lay on top. And there was her father's signet-ring! With a silent prayer of thanks to Castor and Pollux, she slipped the ring and chain into her drawstring coin purse.

Digging deeper, she found three silver bangles and a gold earring. Flavia put these in her purse as well, but decided to leave an assortment of cheap copper chains and earrings; they had gone green with age. With her fingertip she gingerly pushed aside some glittery shards of Alexandrian glass. Beneath them, right at the bottom, lay another earring, which was still bright and yellow. Heavy, too: it was gold. It had three tiny gold chains with a pearl dangling at the end of each, and it was set with a large emerald. Flavia marvelled at its beauty before slipping this earring into her coin purse, too.

Now she must go quickly, before the big magpie returned. She was just about to ease herself down when a noise made her hesitate. It was an odd, panting sound.

She looked nervously at the large tomb a few yards to her right. It was shaped like a small house, with a little arched roof and door. She reckoned it might hold as many as twenty funeral urns, filled with the ashes of the dead.

But the panting did not come from the tomb. It came from directly below her.

Flavia looked down, and her heart skipped a beat. At the foot of the tree were at least half a dozen wild dogs, all staring hungrily up at her!

SCROLL II

Flavia's knees began to tremble uncontrollably. She held onto the tree so tightly her knuckles went white. She must be calm. She must think. Glancing down at the wild dogs again she decided there was only one rational thing to do.

Flavia Gemina screamed.

Although her hands were shaking, she managed to pull herself back up onto a branch. Below her the dogs whined and growled.

'HELP!' she yelled. 'Help me, someone!'

The only response was the rhythmic chirring of cicadas in the afternoon heat.

'Help me!' she shouted, and then, in case someone heard her but didn't think to look up, 'I'm in a tree!'

Most of the dogs were now sitting at the base of the trunk, panting and gazing up at her. They seemed to be smiling at her predicament. There were seven of them, most of them mangy and thin and yellow. The leader was a huge black hound – a mastiff – with evil red eyes and saliva dripping down his hairy chin.

'Stupid dogs!' Flavia muttered under her breath. The leader growled, almost as if he had understood her thoughts.

Suddenly, one of the yellow dogs yelped and leapt to his feet, as if stung by a bee. Then the leader snarled and writhed in pain. A stone had struck him! Flavia saw the next stone fly through the air, and then another, striking with amazing accuracy. The dogs whimpered and yelped and slunk off into the woods.

'Quickly!' a voice called from below. 'Come down quickly before they come back!'

Flavia didn't think twice. She closed her eyes and jumped out of the tree.

'Ouch! My ankle!' Flavia started to run, but a stab of pain shot through her leg and almost made her sick. A boy about her own age ran out from behind a tree. He put his arm awkwardly around her waist and pulled her forward.

'Come *on*!' he urged, and she could see that his dark eyes were full of fear. 'Quickly!'

With each step the pain eased a bit, but they were not moving quickly. They had almost reached the umbrella pine when the boy looked back, stopped, and reached towards his belt.

'Hang on to the tree!' he commanded, pushing Flavia forward. He pulled out his sling, and reached into a leather pouch which hung from his belt. Fitting a sharp stone into the sling he moved a few feet away and swung it quickly round his head. Flavia gripped the tree and closed her eyes. She heard the sling buzz like an angry wasp. Then a dog's yelp and a satisfied 'Got him!' from the boy.

'Come on!' he urged. 'The leader's down but I don't think I killed him. They'll probably be after us in a minute!'

Flavia took a deep breath and moved as quickly as she could. Dry thistles scratched her legs and the boy's strong grip hurt her as he half lifted, half pulled her forward.

Suddenly the boy cried out in a language Flavia had never heard before.

They were nearly at her back door. But the boy was leading her away from it, to the right.

'No! My house is there!' she protested.

The boy ignored her and called out again in his harsh language. He was pulling her to the back door of the house next to hers. He glanced back and muttered something in Latin which Flavia understood perfectly. It was not a polite word.

She heard the dogs barking behind her. The boy pulled her more urgently and she could hear him gasping for breath. The door was closer; now she could see its rough surface beneath the peeling green paint. But by the sound of it, the pack was nearly upon them. At any moment she expected to feel sharp teeth sink into her calf.

Suddenly, the green door swung open. A tall, black-robed figure emerged, pointed at the dogs and bellowed something in an unknown language.

For an instant the dogs stopped dead in their tracks. That instant was enough for the tall figure to grab them both, pull them through the open door and slam it in the dogs' startled faces.

Flavia sobbed with relief. Strong arms held her tight and the rough cloth against her nose smelled spicy and comforting.

Abruptly a dog's cold nose pressed into her armpit. Flavia screamed again and jumped back. A pretty white dog with brown eyes grinned up at her, its entire rear end wagging with delight.

'Bobas! Down! Go away! *Bad* dog!' said the man in black sternly. Bobas took no notice and gave Flavia a long, slobbery kiss.

At this Flavia began to giggle through her tears. This was the dog she had heard barking for the past week, since the mysterious family had moved in to old Festus's house. She sniffed and wiped her runny nose with her arm. Then she stepped back to have a good look at her rescuer.

'Allow me to introduce myself,' said the man in a pleasantly accented voice. 'My name is Mordecai ben Ezra and this is my son Jonathan.' He gave a very slight bow. 'Peace be with you.'

Flavia looked at the boy who had saved her life.

Jonathan was bent over, resting his hands on his knees and breathing hard. He had a rather square face and masses of curly hair. He looked up at her, grinned and also nodded, but seemed unable to speak.

'Miriam!' the boy's father called. 'Bring the oil of marjoram quickly!' And almost apologetically to Flavia: 'My son is somewhat asthmatic.'

Jonathan's father had a sharp nose and a short grizzled beard. Two long grey ringlets of hair emerged from a black turban wound around his head. He looked very exotic and even odd, but his heavy-lidded eyes were kind.

A beautiful girl of about thirteen ran up with a tiny clay jar. She uncorked it and held it under Jonathan's nose.

'This is my daughter Miriam,' said Mordecai proudly. 'Miriam, this is . . .'

They all looked at her.

'Flavia. Flavia Gemina, daughter of Marcus Flavius Geminus, sea captain,' she said, and added: 'Your next door neighbour.'

'Flavia Gemina, will you come into the garden and have a drink and tell us how you came to be pursued by a pack of angry dogs?'

'Yes,' said Flavia, but as she stepped forward, she gasped with pain.

'Your ankle.' Mordecai bent and probed Flavia's swollen right ankle. She winced again, though his fingers were cool and gentle.

'Come. I'm a doctor.' And before she could protest, he had lifted her off her feet and was carrying her in his arms. Jonathan followed, breathing easier now but still holding the oil of marjoram under his nose.

The doctor carried Flavia through a leafy inner garden towards the study. Although the house was laid out exactly like hers, it was a different world. Every surface was covered with multi-coloured carpets and cushions. In the study, instead of a desk and chair, there was a long striped divan going right round the walls. Mordecai set her on this long couch against several embroidered cushions which smelled faintly of some exotic spice: cinnamon, perhaps.

'Miriam, please bring some water, some clean strips of linen and some balm – the Syrian, not the Greek . . .'

'Yes, father,' the girl replied, and then said something in the strange language.

'Please speak Latin in front of our guest,' Mordecai chided gently.

'Yes, father,' she said again, and went out of the room.

'Jonathan,' said the doctor, 'would you prepare some mint tea?'

'Yes, father,' said the boy, breathing easier.

Flavia continued to look round in wonder. There were only three or four shelves of scrolls in her father's study. Here the walls above the divan were covered with them. Nearby, on a carved wooden stand, was the most beautiful open scroll Flavia had ever seen. It was made of creamy, thick parchment and covered with strange black and red letters. Beneath it lay a richly embroidered silk cover of scarlet, blue, gold and black.

Mordecai followed her gaze, then moved over to the scroll.

'We are Jews and this is our holy book,' he said softly. He kissed his fingertips and almost touched the scroll. 'The Torah. I was reading it when I heard my son call.' He rolled it up and reverently slipped it into its silk cover.

Miriam reappeared with a bowl and pitcher, and to Flavia's surprise she began to wash her feet. Jonathan's sister had dark curls like her brother, but her skin was pale and her violet eyes were grave.

While Miriam was drying Flavia's feet, Jonathan came in with four steaming cups on a tray. He handed one to Flavia, who sniffed its minty aroma and gratefully sipped the strong, sweet brew.

Meanwhile, Mordecai applied ointment to her

inflamed ankle and began to bind it securely with strips of linen.

'Tell us your story, please,' he said as he worked.

'Well, I was up in the tree when the dogs came and I knew I could never get past them but your son scared them away and . . and I think he saved my life.' Flavia felt as if she were going to cry again so she took a large gulp of mint tea.

'And may I ask what a Roman girl of good birth was doing up a tree in the middle of a graveyard?' asked Mordecai as he tied off the last strip of linen and patted Flavia's ankle.

'I was looking for the magpie's nest. And I found treasure! I found two gold earrings, and three silver bangles, and got my chain back, and of course my father's . . .' Flavia stopped short. 'Oh no! My father will be worried sick! He has probably sent Caudex out to look for me by now! Oh, I must go home straight away!' She set her cup on a low table.

'Of course,' smiled Mordecai. 'Your ankle was only twisted. It should be fine in a day or two. Jonathan, have you recovered sufficiently to escort this young lady next door?'

'Yes, father,' replied Jonathan.

Together they eased Flavia off the couch and helped her hobble through the atrium. Miriam followed behind. At the front door Flavia turned.

'Goodbye! And thank you! I'm sorry I didn't finish the tea. It was delicious!'

'Peace be with you,' said Mordecai and Miriam together. Each gave a little bow as Jonathan helped Flavia out of the door and along the pavement to her house.

Lifting the familiar bronze knocker of Castor and Pollux, Flavia rapped sharply several times. From deep within she heard Scuto barking and after what seemed like ages the peephole opened and she saw Caudex's bleary eyes staring out. It was a full minute before the sleepy doorkeeper managed to slide the bolt back and pull the door open.

'Pater! *Pater!*' Flavia cried. Jonathan followed curiously as she pushed past Caudex and her bouncing dog. 'Where are you, pater!' she called.

'Here in the study, my dear.' Her father did not sound very worried.

'Pater! I'm here! I've found the ring and I'm safe!' She limped through the folding door, coming up to her father from behind.

Marcus sat bent over the desk, carefully dripping wax on a document.

'And why shouldn't you be safe?' he asked absently, pressing a ring into the hot wax.

'PATER!'

Her father turned round and then jumped to his feet.

'Great Neptune's beard!' he cried. 'What's happened to you? Look at yourself! Your arms are scratched, your hair full of twigs, your tunic torn and dirty, and – and your ankle is bandaged! Whatever happened?'

He peered past her suspiciously.

'And who, may I ask, is this?'

SCROLL III

Ostia, the port of Rome and the town where Flavia lived, was occasionally foggy in the early mornings. And so it was on the morning of Flavia's birthday, three days after she had found the magpie's nest. As a birthday treat, her father had agreed to take her to the goldsmith, to see how much she could get for her little treasure trove.

They left the house shortly after dawn and the mist swirled around them as they walked up Bakers Street towards the river.

'Pater, why can't we go to the town forum? There's a man who buys jewellery there . . .'

'I told you before. You will get a better deal from Aurarius the goldsmith. He is a friend of mine and he will not cheat you, as that perfumed Phoenician in the forum will certainly do. Have you got everything?'

Flavia touched the soft leather coin purse tied to her belt. It contained the objects she had found in the magpie's nest. She was hoping to sell them and buy a set of all twelve scrolls of the *Aeneid*, a book she had always wanted. She had recently seen a set in the forum at the bookseller's stall. It was a beautiful parchment version with illustrations. But the bookseller was asking a vast sum: one hundred sesterces. Flavia hardly dared hope the jewellery in her purse would fetch that amount.

They crossed the Decumanus Maximus carefully. Because it was the town's main street as well as the road to Rome, it was usually covered with horse and donkey dung. There were no handy stepping stones, as in some other Roman towns, but Flavia and her father crossed without mishap. They passed the theatre and the forum of the corporations on their left and stopped to press themselves against the wall of a tavern as a mule-drawn cart rattled down the narrow street.

As they approached the river, the fog grew thicker and damper. The tops of the tall brick warehouses were not even visible as they passed beneath them. Flavia shivered and pulled her woollen cloak closer around her shoulders. Ostia had three harbours: a little marina for Ostia's fishing boats, pleasure craft and smaller merchantmen, a large harbour for the massive grain ships from Egypt, and the river harbour between the two. Here vessels could unload and either have their cargoes towed by barge up to Rome or stored in warehouses. Flavia and her father turned left at the river and walked past these warehouses as they made for Aurarius's workshop.

Above her, unseen gulls wheeled and cried peevishly in the fog, and she heard the creak of timber and clink of ships' tackle to her right. The wooden quay was damp beneath her leather boots.

Figures loomed up out of the mist, terrifying men with broken noses, mangled ears and meaty arms. Some had lost arms or hands or legs. But their ugly faces always broke into grins when they saw her father, and they invariably greeted him politely.

Suddenly, Flavia heard a sound which chilled her blood: the crack of a whip and clink of chains. Out of the mist emerged a pitiful sight: a line of women, naked and chained at the neck. Most of them seemed to be Egyptian or Syrian, but one or two were dark-skinned Africans. Their heads had been shaved and they were terribly thin. Some had open sores.

Flavia could hear their teeth chattering, but otherwise they were totally silent. Apart from their iron collars and chains, they wore nothing but crude wooden tags with prices scrawled on them.

The whip cracked again and out of the mist came the person Flavia feared most in the world: Venalicius, the slave-dealer. There were many rumours about Venalicius, the most recent that he had kidnapped a nine-year-old girl named Sapphira and sold her to a Syrian merchant. This was illegal, but once a child had fallen into Venalicius' hands and his ship had sailed, there was virtually no way of ever finding the child again, or of proving the slave-dealer's guilt.

Venalicius had one blind eye: a horrible, milky orb that sat in its socket like a peeled egg. His teeth were rotten and his nose sprouted tufts of mouldy hair. Worst of all, one ear was missing, bitten off by a slave he had afterwards crucified, if the rumour was true. The wound still seeped a horrible yellow pus. Once, Venalicius had whispered to Flavia when her father wasn't looking: 'I'll make a slave of you, too, my dear, if I ever catch you!'

Flavia shivered again and averted her eyes. But just as she did, she noticed a figure at the end of the line. It was a dark-skinned girl about her own age. She was not weeping, but her beautiful amber eyes looked blank with despair. Her hands hung limp by her side, not bothering to cover her nakedness. Around her neck – beneath the iron collar – hung a wooden plaque with six C's scrawled crudely upon it.

'Six hundred,' whispered Flavia to herself.

In a moment the girl had disappeared along with the others into the mist, as Venalicius drove them into town.

Flavia and her father moved silently on, both subdued by the sight of the slaves.

'Pater, what will happen to them?' Flavia asked presently.

'You know what happens to slaves,' her father replied quietly. 'Those women don't look terribly healthy and unless they speak Latin they'll end up doing menial work: cleaning, sewing . . . Perhaps some of them will become cooks, if they're lucky.'

'Like Alma?'

'Yes, like your nurse Alma.'

'Pater . . .' Flavia took a deep breath: 'Pater, what will happen to the girl?'

There was such a long pause she thought he would not answer her. Her father guided her carefully around a mound of silver fish spilling from a yellow net. Then:

'She may become a lady's maid. Or a cook's assistant. Or perhaps someone will buy her for a wife,' he said quietly.

'A wife!' cried Flavia in horror. 'But she's my age!'

'Perhaps a bit older. You know that eleven or twelve is not too old for slaves to marry.'

Flavia said nothing more until they reached Aurarius's shop. It was at the end of a row of brick workshops built against one of the large warehouses along the waterfront. Tatters of fog swirled around the shop and the roof of the warehouse above it was swallowed in the mist.

The goldsmith Aurarius – a wizened, slightly cross-eyed man – looked up from his charcoal brazier and greeted them cheerfully. A big watchdog dozed at his feet.

The smith examined the contents of Flavia's pouch with interest.

'Hmmm. The bangles are nice but not worth more than two or three sesterces. This earring is lovely. It's made of electrum. Mixture of gold and silver which can be melted down. I'll give you a hundred and fifty sesterces for it . . .'

He emptied the last object from the purse into his palm and his eyes widened. He glanced up at Flavia's father and then brought the earring almost to the tip of his nose.

'This one with the emerald is really special,' he said. 'Pure gold, maybe Greek manufacture, and one of the finest stones I've ever seen. Too bad you don't have its mate. The pair would be worth eight or nine hundred sesterces. But on its own I could only offer you four hundred . . .'

He looked gravely at Flavia.

'Your father's done me many favours, so tell you what: I'll give you six hundred sesterces for all four pieces. It's a fair price. You won't get better.'

'I'll take it,' said Flavia immediately, and held out a trembling hand to receive six gold coins, each worth a hundred sesterces. It was an enormous sum.

Flavia's heart was pounding as she slipped the coins into her pouch. She turned to her father.

'Pater, may we go to the forum right away? I know what I want to buy for my birthday.'

The mist cleared as they made their way to the central town forum and the soft blue sky promised a perfect day. Flavia walked quickly through the fish market, past fishmongers boasting loudly about their red mullet, sole and squid. She hurried past the fruit-sellers who were hawking their pomegranates, melons and peaches; past the jewellery stall, the toy stall, the pottery stall and the clothes stall. She did not even glance at the book stall as she passed. As they entered the forum, she walked so fast that her father had to hurry to keep up with her.

By the time Flavia Gemina approached the slave stall she was almost running. She looked around anxiously and then let out her breath.

'Thank goodness, she's still there!'

Wedged between a banker's stall and a public scribe's, in the shadow of the temple of Rome and Augustus, was a slightly raised wooden stage. The slave women she had seen earlier stood on this platform while Venalicius strutted up and down before them, shouting out their virtues. Already a crowd was gathering to look and prod and poke the slaves, who were still completely naked.

'How can they treat them like that? Like animals,' murmured Flavia. Untying her coin purse, she began to move forward.

Her father's firm hand on her shoulder stopped her short.

'Let me handle this,' he warned. 'Venalicius might try to take advantage of you. He can smell a serious buyer from half a mile away. He might raise his price or even double it.'

'He can't *do* that! Can he?'

'He can do whatever he likes until she is sold,' replied her father gravely. 'Keep back. Out of sight.'

Flavia handed the leather purse to her father and stepped back behind one of the marble pillars of the colonnade. Captain Geminus pushed through the crowd and began to walk casually up and down the line. Flavia noticed that the price for the girl was double the price of most of the other women, and she shivered in the morning sunshine.

'Ah, the young sea captain: Marcus Flavius Geminus! Are you a serious buyer, or just looking?' sneered Venalicius. Flavia saw her father's back stiffen, but he moved on quietly.

'How much is this one?' she heard him ask as he stopped in front of a red-eyed young woman in her late teens.

'Three hundred sesterces. Can't you read?' snapped the slave-dealer.

Another man, a soldier, had stopped in front of the girl. Flavia held her breath. She saw the soldier reach out and open the girl's mouth to examine her teeth. Then he bent and peered at the price round her neck. He stood again and looked at the girl, who stared straight ahead. Flavia's fingernails dug into her palm.

Abruptly, the soldier shook his head and moved on. Flavia slowly let out her breath in a huge sigh of relief. 'Hurry, pater!' she whispered to herself.

As the soldier walked off, her father indicated the girl and said calmly to Venalicius, 'I'll take this one please.'

'Just a moment,' smirked the slave-dealer, 'I'm dealing with another customer.' He made a great pretence of helping a fat merchant in a grubby toga who was examining another woman.

That slave-dealer is torturing me on purpose! thought Flavia to herself. And then: oh please, Castor and Pollux, let me be able to buy her.

After what seemed like ages the fat merchant turned away, making a joke to a friend. The two of them went off laughing. Venalicius turned at last to her father.

'Yes, Captain Geminus?'

'I'd like to buy this girl,' repeated her father.

The slave-dealer raised his ugly head and seemed to look around the crowded marketplace with his horrible blind eye. Flavia ducked back behind the marble column and pressed her cheek against its reassuring solidness.

Then she heard Venalicius say very clearly to her father, 'The African girl costs seven hundred sesterces.'

SCROLL IV

The price-tag around the slave-girl's neck read six hundred, but now Venalicius was asking for seven! Flavia wanted to shout that it wasn't fair. Instead, she bit her lip and swallowed her protest. Tears blurred her vision. She had been so close to saving the girl. So close to having someone her own age to be with. So close to . . .

'Very well,' she heard her father say in a matter-of-fact voice. 'Here you are.'

Flavia did not dare break the spell by looking. She shut her eyes tight and held her breath.

A minute later she heard the slave-dealer call out mockingly: 'I hope she serves you well, Captain!'

Flavia opened her eyes and peeked around the column. Her father was moving through the crowd, and the girl was with him. Flavia ran to meet them.

'Pater! The extra hundred sesterces! The gold in my bag was only worth six hundred!'

'I paid the extra amount.'

'But so much, pater!'

'You are forgetting that today is special. Happy birthday, my dear.'

Flavia threw her arms round her father and hugged him tightly. She wanted to hug the girl, too, and tell her everything was going to be all right now, but something about the slave-girl's empty look stopped her. Instead Flavia slipped off her cloak and gently wrapped it around the girl's naked body.

Then they took her home.

Later that morning, Flavia made an important discovery: the slave-girl she had bought spoke no Latin, and only a little Greek.

The girl had said nothing on the way home, or when Flavia had bathed the sores on her neck with a sea sponge and applied some of Mordecai's soothing aloe balm. But after Flavia had taken her up to her bedroom and dressed her in a soft yellow tunic, the girl had looked up timidly at Flavia and recited in a faltering voice:

'Greetings. My name is Nubia. How may I please you?'

'Hello, Nubia! I'm Flavia Gemina, daughter of Marcus Flavius Geminus, sea captain!'

Nubia looked at her blankly and then repeated: 'Greetings. My name is Nubia. How may I please you?'

Flavia realised the girl didn't understand the words she was reciting. She probably didn't know any Latin at all.

'Flavia,' said Flavia slowly, pointing at herself. 'I am Flavia.'

'Flavia,' repeated Nubia haltingly.

'Yes! Are you hungry, Nubia?'

Nubia looked blank. Flavia opened her mouth and pointed inside. The girl started back with horror.

Flavia pretended to chew something.

Nubia's eyes lit up and she nodded.

'Come on then! Let's go down to the kitchen and see what Alma is cooking!' Flavia quickly reached for Nubia's hand but the girl drew back with a frightened expression.

Flavia remembered that when she first got Scuto he also cringed at any sudden movement. Her father said it was because he had been beaten.

'Don't be afraid! Come!' said Flavia and moved slowly towards the doorway of her bedroom.

Nubia followed hesitantly as they went down the wooden stairs, past the sunny garden, and into the small kitchen.

Alma, Flavia's former nursemaid, had recently taken over kitchen duties. The previous cook, Gusto, had died shopping for leeks in the forum when a donkey kicked him in the head.

Alma had proved to be an excellent cook, and was daily growing plumper from sampling her own recipes. She was tasting something at that very moment, leaning over the glowing ashes on the kitchen hearth with a spoon half poised above a steaming pan. Flavia greeted her and then introduced Nubia.

'Alma, this is Nubia. Nubia, this is Alma: she used to be my nurse.'

'Welcome, Nubia,' beamed the cook. Normally she would have thrown her arms around such a sad-looking creature and given her a warm embrace, but she had been alerted to treat the new slave gently. Even Scuto had been shut away in the storeroom for the time being.

'I'm just cooking your birthday dinner,' said Alma, 'so I can't stop to chat. But I've prepared some fruit and bread. Take it into the garden.' She handed Flavia a platter laid out with various fruits and a flat round loaf of bread.

Nubia pointed to a date and said 'date' very softly in Greek.

'Yes! That's the Greek word for date!' said Flavia. 'Do you understand Greek? Do you want a date?' And then in Greek, 'Take one!'

Nubia looked at her in awe and disbelief. Slowly she reached out her hand and took a date. She closed her eyes as she ate it and a look of pure delight passed over her lovely face.

'Have much.' Flavia's Greek was not very fluent. She had only been studying it for two years. Now she wished she had worked harder at it.

'Have big date!' she tried again. Nubia understood and solemnly took another date.

'Let's go . . . garden,' said Flavia, when she had remembered the Greek word for garden. She led the way to her favourite seat by the fountain.

Nubia stared in amazement at the spout of water shooting up from the copper pipe in the centre of the marble basin. Slowly she put her finger in it, then quickly withdrew it as if she had been burned.

'Water!' she said in Greek, and then, 'I drink?'

'Yes! You can drink it!' cried Flavia in delight. And demonstrated the fact.

Nubia drank, too, for a long time and then turned back to the plate. They sat on the marble bench, and together they named the foods: bread, date, peach, grapes, apples. Then Nubia set down to eating in earnest. She had two pieces of bread, a bunch of grapes, half an apple and a whole peach. Finally she ate up every date on the plate.

'You like dates?' said Flavia.

'Yes like dates,' replied Nubia with her mouth quite full.

'Better stop. Enough,' said Flavia in Greek. And then, reverting to Latin, 'I'm having a birthday dinner party in a few hours and there will be lots of delicious food. Jonathan from next door is coming, and his father Mordecai and his sister Miriam and my father, of course, and you're coming too, so don't eat too much.'

Nubia gazed solemnly at Flavia.

'Lots more later good food,' said Flavia in Greek,

with a sigh, and wished again that she had paid more attention during lessons with her tutor Aristo.

Flavia was determined that her birthday dinner party would be a success. Her plan was to have Nubia recline next to Miriam, who seemed so quiet and gentle. She herself would lie on the same couch as Jonathan, and her father and Mordecai would take the third couch.

'No,' said her father firmly, 'I'm afraid it's no good.'

'Why not, pater?'

'First of all, you're not old enough to recline at dinner yet . . .'

Flavia started to protest but he held up his hand and smiled.

'If it were just a family gathering, I would let you recline. But it's not. Furthermore, you told me our next door neighbours are foreigners. From Judaea, was it?'

Flavia nodded.

'Well, they might not feel comfortable reclining. Better to sit, don't you think, my little owl?' He ruffled her hair affectionately.

'Yes, pater,' she sighed.

'Also,' said Captain Geminus, 'did you know that when a mistress invites her slave to recline, it means she is granting that slave her freedom?'

Flavia shook her head.

'At least wait until Nubia has learned enough Latin to find her way around Ostia before you set her free,' he said with a smile.

So Flavia modified her plan and her seating arrangement.

The six of them sat around a large oval table which Caudex and her father had carried in from the atrium. Flavia seated Nubia next to Miriam, and was glad to see Jonathan's sister give the African girl a warm smile.

When her guests were seated, Flavia handed out garlands of ivy and violets which she had made herself. Mordecai balanced his garland on top of his white turban and didn't seem to mind when Jonathan and Flavia giggled at him.

Captain Geminus poured the wine, well-watered for the children, and they all toasted Flavia's health. Nubia wrinkled her pretty nose when she first tasted the wine, but soon took another sip.

After the toast there was an awkward silence. The doctor sat stiffly in a green silk kaftan while her father fiddled with the folds of his toga. Flavia glanced anxiously towards the kitchen, wondering what was keeping Alma. Jonathan whistled a little tune under his breath and then winked at Flavia.

Finally, Alma proudly carried in the first course and set it on the table: sea snails fried in olive oil, garlic and pepper. The snails had been placed back in their shells and Alma handed each diner a special spoon with a small hook at one end to extract the snail.

'Are we permitted to eat these, father?' whispered Jonathan, gazing in dismay at the creatures.

'God has made all things clean,' his father murmured, and politely took a snail.

Flavia showed Jonathan how to extract a snail and then watched as he gingerly picked up one of the shells between finger and thumb and hooked out its contents. He paused to examine it: the snail was small and twisted and rubbery and brown. Jonathan closed his eyes, took a deep breath and put it in his mouth.

He chewed.

He opened his eyes.

He smiled.

'Mmmm!' he beamed, and eagerly finished off the rest. Under the stern gaze of her father, Miriam also made a brave attempt. Nubia, imitating Flavia to see how it was done, ate up every snail on her plate.

Jonathan wiped his hands on his tunic, which already had a dribble of garlic oil down the front. Then he drained his wine cup with a smack of his lips. Nubia, watching him carefully, also wiped her hands on her tunic and smacked as she drained her wine cup.

Flavia smiled.

'For our next course we're having dormice

stuffed with chopped sows' udders,' she announced brightly.

Mordecai and his children froze in horror.

Nubia looked blank.

'Flavia . . .' said her father with a warning look.

'Just joking,' giggled Flavia. 'My favourite food is really roast chicken. You do like roast chicken, don't you?'

After that the party perked up nicely. Everyone relaxed and laughed and ate up their roast chicken and told stories about the most revolting food they had ever been offered.

Mordecai had once found a sheep's eyeball in his stew while dining with a camel trader in Judaea. Flavia's father had devoured a delicious fish soup in the port of Massilia and discovered a rotten fish head at the bottom of his bowl. Just last week, Miriam had deeply offended her host by refusing to eat three roast quail whose tiny charred heads dangled woefully. And Flavia swore she knew a baker who added chalk and sand to his flour, in order to cut costs.

But Jonathan's experience beat them all. Once, when chewing a mouthful of meat pie bought from a street vendor in Rome, his tongue had encountered something tough and gristly. Pulling it out of his mouth to inspect it, he had discovered, to his horror, that it was the tip of someone's finger.

Everyone groaned and pushed their plates away. Luckily they had finished the main course. Captain Geminus refilled empty wine cups and presently Alma came in with the dessert course: dates and slices of sugary pink watermelon.

Jonathan, who was becoming slightly tipsy, pretended that two dates were his eyes and a slice of watermelon his grinning mouth. Flavia giggled and Nubia smiled for the first time.

Encouraged by the success of this antic, Jonathan stuck a leftover snail up each nostril. Flavia snorted with laughter, Nubia giggled and Miriam rolled her eyes. Mordecai cleared his throat.

'With your permission, I think it's time for us to take our leave,' he said, with a significant glance at his son.

'But first, happy birthday, Flavia. This is from us all.' He reached under his chair and brought out a fat leather cylinder tied with a scarlet ribbon.

Flavia knew immediately that it was a scroll case. With excited fingers she opened the leather top and pulled out one of the scrolls inside.

'It's not new, I'm afraid,' said Mordecai in his accented voice. 'To tell the truth I have two sets, so I thought I could spare this one.'

Flavia's eyes opened wide with delight as she unrolled the papyrus. 'It's the *Aeneid*. It's the very thing I wanted. And look at the beautiful illustrations!'

Everyone pushed back their chairs and crowded around to look at the scroll and admire the pictures.

'Flavia?' prompted her father. 'What do you say?'

'Oh! Thank you Doctor Mordecai, Jonathan, Miriam. It's such a generous gift. Thank you!' And then: 'Look, Nubia! I can help you learn Latin by reading this story to you.'

But Nubia was not in her chair. She had vanished.

SCROLL V

'Oh no, I knew it would all be too much for her!' cried Flavia. 'She only came off the slave ship this morning!'

'Don't worry,' said Mordecai. 'Perhaps the food was too rich for her. She may be in the latrine.'

But when Flavia reported that Nubia wasn't there, they all began to worry and decided to search the house.

Still wearing their party garlands, Mordecai and Flavia's father looked downstairs, while Jonathan, Miriam and Flavia searched the upstairs bedrooms. The doorkeeper Caudex, dozing in the atrium, swore that no one had gone out. Alma, scrubbing plates in the kitchen, had the back door constantly in her line of sight. She was sure Nubia had not gone near it.

When they had searched the whole house they met in the atrium by the household shrine.

'Before we begin the search outside,' said Flavia's father, gravely removing his garland, 'have we checked every room?'

'Yes,' said the children.

'Yes,' nodded Mordecai.

'No,' said Caudex slowly, scratching his armpit.

They all gazed at the big slave.

'Scuto is still shut up in the storeroom,' he mumbled. 'He was whining and scratching to be let out but – '

'Yes?' they cried.

'Then he went very quiet.'

They all hurried to the storeroom and cautiously Captain Geminus opened the door. By now it was dusk and the storeroom, which had no windows, was dim and shadowy. They could just make out the shapes of dozens of storage jars full of wine and grain, half-buried in the sandy earth to keep them from toppling over.

'I think I see him,' said Flavia's father. 'Bring a lamp.'

Alma rushed to hand him a clay oil-lamp and the captain stepped into the storeroom.

'Great Neptune's beard!' he exclaimed softly.

In the golden lamplight they saw Nubia and Scuto curled up asleep on the sandy floor. The girl's dark head rested on the dog's broad, woolly back. She had placed her flowered garland on his head. As they all crowded into the doorway, Scuto raised his big head, with the garland slightly askew. He looked at them drowsily, sighed deeply and went back to sleep.

⋆

One bright afternoon, a few days later, Flavia's new friends accompanied her to the river harbour to see her father off on a voyage.

Doctor Mordecai and Captain Geminus led the way.

They looked an unlikely pair, Flavia thought, as she watched them walking and talking together: her fair-haired Roman father in his tunic and blue cloak, the doctor with his exotic turban, robe and beard. But they had a common passion: travel. Mordecai had lived in Babylon and Jerusalem, two cities her father had never visited, and Captain Geminus had seen many countries which Mordecai had only read about.

Flavia was glad they liked each other because in only a few days she and Jonathan had also become firm friends.

Jonathan had been coming to her house every morning to help teach Nubia Latin. He and Flavia had been reading the *Aeneid* to her, often stopping to explain or act out words. Jonathan was very funny and made them both laugh. Flavia thought it was good for Nubia to laugh.

Now, as they made their way towards the River Tiber, Nubia was walking between Flavia and Jonathan, holding Scuto's lead. Since the night of the dinner party, the slave-girl and the dog had been inseparable. She even refused to sleep in the new bed they had brought up to Flavia's room. Instead,

Nubia curled up every night in the garden with Scuto, and slept under the stars.

Also walking with them to the docks was her father's patron, Titus Cordius Atticus, who had chartered her father's ship for a two-week voyage to Greece. He intended to visit the town of Corinth to buy pottery, perfume and bronzes.

Cordius was a very wealthy merchant who lived opposite them, in one of the largest and most beautiful houses in Ostia. He also had a town house in Rome and an estate in Sicily. But despite his wealth he always seemed very sad.

Flavia's father had once told her the reason: while Cordius had been serving as a officer in Germania, his whole family had been slaughtered by barbarians. A lovely wife, three fine young sons and a baby girl, now all gone to the underworld, and no one to leave his great riches to.

'Cordius doesn't need to work as a merchant,' her father had said, 'but since he lost his family there is a deep restlessness in him. I think he travels to get away from his empty houses. All the wealth in the world is no good if you don't have a family.' Her father had hugged her tightly.

Recently, however, Cordius had seemed more cheerful. Sometimes his stern face even relaxed into a smile. Flavia knew why, but she had been sworn to secrecy: Cordius was considering adopting his young freedman Libertus. She had overheard the rich merchant discussing it with her father.

'You mustn't tell a soul,' Flavia's father had warned her. 'He is still thinking about it and no one knows, not even Libertus.'

Previously a slave in Cordius's household, Libertus had shown such skill and promise that he had been set free. Now a freedman, he still lived and worked in his patron's house, but was paid for it.

Flavia considered that Libertus would make some girl a fine husband. He had straight black hair, clear skin and dark blue eyes. He was young, intelligent and charming. Furthermore, if Cordius adopted Libertus, one day he would be incredibly wealthy.

And so Flavia was delighted to see Libertus walking beside Jonathan's sister Miriam. She thought they made a dazzling couple and wondered if the young freedman was telling Miriam that her eyes were like amethysts and her skin like alabaster. Then she heard him say something about 'slavery in Judaea', and sighed. Libertus was definitely not wooing Miriam.

As they emerged from between two warehouses and stepped onto the quayside, Flavia took a deep breath of the salty air. Seagulls and swifts soared and swooped above the river. Sailors and dockers rolled barrels and wine jars, slaves loaded crates on carts, and soldiers marched past. And this was the quietest time of day.

The harbour always made Flavia feel both excited and sad. Excited because every ship promised a new adventure, sad because her father so often went away.

The sight of her father's small ship, the *Myrtilla*, also made Flavia sad. Myrtilla had been the name of her mother, who had died in childbirth when Flavia was only three years old. The twin baby boys had died, too. Flavia had been left alone with only her father and nurse Alma.

As they approached the *Myrtilla*'s berth, three burly Phoenician brothers shouted their greetings from various parts of the ship. They were called Quartus, Quintus and Sextus. The fourth crew member was an Ethiopian named Ebenus. His oiled, cheerful face rose up from the hold when he heard the others.

Her father and the merchant Cordius had already stowed their belongings on board the ship. They had visited the temple of Castor and Pollux, to make sacrifice for a good and profitable journey. Now, the wind was favourable and it was time for them to depart.

Captain Geminus bounded up the boarding plank to make some last-minute checks aboard the ship, while Cordius gave Libertus some final instructions. Flavia was disappointed to see the handsome freedman hurry home shortly afterwards. She noticed Miriam watching Libertus until he was out of sight.

Suddenly, Flavia noticed that Nubia had begun to tremble uncontrollably. The docks obviously upset her. The slave-girl hugged Scuto for reassurance and his wet kisses seemed to calm her.

A few moments later, Captain Geminus came down the boarding plank and put one arm around Flavia's shoulder.

'Time for me to go,' he said with a smile, and then added gravely, 'you know, I'm a little worried about your safety since that incident with the dogs. Your tutor isn't here to look out for you this month, Caudex can be terribly slow and I don't know what Alma would do to protect you against a pack of wild dogs, or even kidnappers . . .'

'Don't worry, pater. I'm not alone. Doctor Mordecai lives next door and I have Jonathan and Nubia to keep me company now. And there's Scuto.'

'Ah yes. The fierce watchdog.'

They looked down at Scuto, who was lathering Nubia's face with his wet tongue. Smiling, Captain Geminus shook his head.

'Well, if I hear you've been in the least danger, I'm packing you off to my brother's the next time I go on a voyage!'

'Don't worry, pater. Jonathan and I will sit quietly in the garden all day and take turns reading the *Aeneid* to Nubia. We're teaching her Latin.' She pulled Nubia close and put a protective arm around her.

'Good, good . . .' Flavia's father quickly kissed her on the top of her head, said goodbye to the rest of them and then he and Cordius boarded the ship.

Using oars, the crew soon manoeuvred the small ship out of her berth and into the river channel. As the swift current carried the *Myrtilla* down towards the river mouth, Flavia's father stood at the helm, holding the steering paddle.

Although Flavia usually stayed to watch until the *Myrtilla* passed right out of sight, Nubia was trembling again, so Flavia decided to take her home quickly. Her father was busy at the helm, but just before they started back Flavia saw him turn and wave one last time.

It was still early afternoon when they returned to Green Fountain Street. Theirs was one of the few quiet residential streets in the bustling town, and now, at the hottest time of the day, it was almost deserted: only Libertus stood at the communal fountain in the middle of the crossroads. They waved as they walked past, and Flavia noticed Miriam give him a shy smile.

As soon as they had left the docks, Nubia had stopped trembling. Now, Jonathan was walking beside her and teaching her words in Latin by pointing at objects and saying their names.

'Door,' he said.

'Door,' she repeated.

'Lion.' He indicated a bronze door-knocker.

'Lion.'

'Kerb.'

'Kerb.'

'Fountain.'

'Fountain. Water?'

'Yes! Water! Good!' encouraged Jonathan.
'Street.'

'Street.'

'Don't step in that!'

'Don't step . . .?'

'Well, that looks like horse dung, but people empty their chamber pots here and it's pretty wet so I think we'd better go back on the pavement.'

Nubia looked at him solemnly.

'Pavement,' said Jonathan

'Pavement,' repeated Nubia.

'And what's this? Blood?'

'Blood,' said Nubia, and pointed at the trail of drops that led to Jonathan's front door.

SCROLL VI

The spots of blood, each about the size of a small coin, were a startling and vivid red. Flavia stooped to touch one, but Jonathan ran ahead, following the drops to his front door.

'Father, the door's open!' he called over his shoulder.

'Don't go in,' shouted Mordecai, 'there may be robbers still in the house!'

But he was too late. Jonathan had disappeared inside. Mordecai and Miriam hurried forward.

As they reached the door, Jonathan stepped back out, his face drained of all colour. He looked at them silently for a moment and then bent over and was sick in the road.

'Stay back, everyone,' began Mordecai in alarm, but Miriam had already pushed past him. Her scream broke the stillness of the afternoon.

'He's dead,' they heard her sob.

Mordecai rushed after her into the house. Flavia, Nubia and Scuto all moved forward to follow him, but Jonathan's arm – surprisingly strong – blocked their way.

'It's our watchdog Bobas,' he said quietly. 'You don't want to look. Someone has cut off his head and taken it away.'

'Who else was in your house?' asked Flavia an hour later.

She and Nubia were sitting with Jonathan in her garden, trying to comfort him. Miriam had been so upset by the bloodstain on the floor that Mordecai had taken her across town to stay with relatives for a few days.

Nubia had one arm around Scuto's neck. They had managed to make her understand what had happened to Bobas and she seemed determined to protect Scuto from a similar fate.

'No one else was in our house,' Jonathan answered grimly.

'What about the slaves?'

'We don't have any slaves. My father doesn't think it right to keep them.'

'But you told me your mother died when you were very young. Don't you even have a nursemaid or cook?'

'No. It's just the three of us.'

'Who does your cleaning?' gasped Flavia in amazement.

'I do,' replied Jonathan, almost proudly. 'And I garden. Miriam does the shopping and a little cooking. And Bobas was our doorkeeper and protector . . .' He bit his lip, and Flavia said quickly:

'Was anything stolen?'

'No. After we buried Bobas's body in the garden we looked everywhere. But nothing is missing. In fact, I found this in the atrium, not far from his body . . .' He held out a little quartz cube with circles scratched on its surface. Nubia took it from his hand and looked at it in puzzlement.

'What this?' asked Nubia.

'It's one of a pair of dice,' explained Flavia. She mimed throwing it and said in Greek: 'For gambling. For money.'

'It's not ours,' said Jonathan. 'My father would be very upset if he ever found me or my sister gambling,'

'Keep it safe,' said Flavia, handing it back to him, 'it may be a clue.' She looked up at the fig tree thoughtfully.

'If nothing was stolen, why did they kill Bobas?'

'Well . . .' Jonathan began, and then stopped. He pulled a twig off a bush and scratched idly at the ground.

'Why? Tell me,' insisted Flavia. She thought of pretty Bobas, with his lovely brown eyes and friendly nature.

'We . . . you've probably guessed that we are different from you. We have a different religion.'

'You're Jewish, aren't you?' said Flavia. Jonathan nodded.

'The people where we used to live didn't like us. That's why we moved here, to the edge of town, where no one would know who we were . . . where no one would bother us. Our old neighbours wrote things on the wall of our house and once they threw rotten eggs at father.'

'Do you think your old neighbours killed Bobas?'

'Maybe . . .' shrugged Jonathan. He seemed reluctant to talk about it.

'Why do they hate you so much?' Flavia asked. 'There are many Jews here in Ostia. I've seen their temple down by the docks.'

'Synagogue,' corrected Jonathan quietly and continued to scratch at the ground. It was obvious the subject made him uncomfortable.

'Well, I intend to solve this crime,' announced Flavia firmly. 'Whoever did this is wicked and should be caught.'

Nubia had been listening to their conversation attentively. Now she surprised them both by saying vehemently:

'Bad man. Kill dog. Find him.' Her amber eyes blazed with passion and she was squeezing Scuto's neck so tightly that he whimpered and rolled his eyes at her.

Flavia looked at Nubia and then turned to Jonathan.

'Do you want to find the person who killed your dog?' she asked him.

He looked up at her, and his eyes were blazing, too. 'Yes.'

'Then it's settled,' said Flavia calmly. 'We will solve this mystery and together we will find the killer.'

Flavia decided that they should begin their quest for justice by interviewing possible witnesses.

Wax tablet in hand and flanked by Jonathan and Nubia, she began in the kitchen. Alma assured them that she had heard nothing suspicious while they were out, though she did remark that Bobas barked so often she barely noticed it.

Next they looked for Caudex. They found him in the garden, snipping the dead heads off roses. When questioned, he confessed he had been dozing.

'Just a little nap in my room as I usually have after lunch,' he admitted, and after a pause, 'I could easily have heard if anyone had knocked on our door.'

The only other possible witness was Libertus, Cordius's freedman. Flavia remembered that he had been standing by the fountain on the corner when they had returned from the river harbour.

They caught Libertus just as he left the house, on his way to the baths.

'Around noon?' he said, as they fell into step beside him. 'Yes, as a matter of fact I did see someone. It was just before you came back from the harbour. I was drinking at the fountain and a man went running past. He looked very frightened and he was carrying a leather bag. I distinctly remember the leather bag. For some reason it reminded me of Perseus with the head of Medusa.'

'What Perseus?' whispered Nubia to Flavia.

'Perseus was a hero who had to kill a monster named Medusa. He cut off her head,' Flavia made a chopping motion with her hand, 'and he put it out of sight in a bag.' She mimed that, too, and then added in Greek: 'In myth. Monster's head in bag.'

Nubia understood: 'Perseus killed.'

'Yes, Perseus killed her.' Flavia turned back to the freedman. 'Libertus,' she said gravely, 'today someone killed Jonathan's watchdog and cut off its head. The head is still missing.'

'By Hercules!' gasped Libertus, and stopped dead in his tracks. 'That is exactly the impression I got: of a head in a bag.'

'What did the man look like?' Jonathan asked.

Libertus shrugged and began walking again. 'Just average, really. Clean-shaven, medium height, light tunic, short dark cloak – I can't remember much more than that.'

They were approaching the centre of town and the streets were becoming more crowded. They all stood back to let a man pushing a handcart full of melons go past.

'I really must hurry,' said Libertus. 'I'm meeting someone at the baths . . .'

'Just one more question,' said Flavia. 'Do you remember which way he went at the crossroads: to the port, to the graves or towards the forum?'

'Yes, I do recall that,' said Libertus, frowning pensively. 'I remember I thought it curious at the time. He was running towards the tombs.'

It was the hottest time of the day. Hidden in the sun-bleached grasses of the necropolis, the cicadas made their sleepy creaking noise. Flavia, Jonathan and Nubia – with Scuto romping ahead – proceeded somewhat fearfully along a dirt road flanked by cypress trees and tombs.

Although their houses backed directly onto the graveyard, they had approached by means of the gate and road that the running man must have taken. The road was not much used and the tombs on either side of it were overgrown and untended.

Here and there were the usual piles of rubbish that accumulated outside the gates of any Roman town: pottery shards, old sandals, broken furniture and clothes too tattered for the secondhand stall.

'What about the wild dogs who attacked us a few days ago?' Flavia looked around nervously. 'I don't want to meet them again.'

'I've been hunting lots of times in the graveyard and that was the only time I've seen them. We'll just have to take the risk. Besides,' Jonathan added, 'we want to find clues while they are fresh.'

As they walked, they looked right and left and especially down, for any telltale drops of blood. Scuto, who had begun by running back and forth to smell interesting smells, was now plodding down the middle of the road with his tail down, panting in the afternoon heat. Suddenly he stopped, looked to his left and wagged his tail.

'Over there,' said Jonathan, pointing. 'He sees something.' Scuto, tail still wagging, led them through the tombs to a small clearing among the pine and cypress trees. Beside a miniature tomb lit by dappled sunlight sat a man with short dark hair and a pale yellow tunic. He sat cross-legged with his back to them, and they could hear sobs and see his shoulders trembling.

As they came nearer, the man heard them and turned. His face was red with crying and his mouth turned down like an actor's tragic mask. Heavy eyebrows joined above his nose to form one dark line. Flavia had never seen such misery before.

But his misery turned to rage when he saw the little group. He rose to his feet and pointing a finger at Scuto he screamed:

'Get that animal away from me. Get him away or I'll kill him. I hate dogs. I hate them all!'

SCROLL VII

The weeping man wiped his nose angrily on his arm and then bent down. He picked up a pine cone, drew back his arm, and threw it at Scuto. It fell short and the man sobbed again, 'Get away!'

He began looking around for other missiles but the three of them had already turned and were running back towards the road. Scuto loped behind them, still wagging his tail as if it were a game.

'Is the man following us?' gasped Flavia when they reached the road again.

'No, I don't think so,' said Jonathan. He was wheezing a bit. While she waited for him to catch his breath, Flavia joined Nubia in patting Scuto.

'Don't worry, Scuto,' she said in a soothing voice, 'we won't let the bad man get you.'

'Not bad man,' said Nubia.

Flavia and Jonathan both looked up at her in surprise.

'Sad man,' said Nubia quietly.

'But that's probably the man who killed Bobas!' Jonathan cried.

'You may be right,' agreed Flavia.

'But how can we be sure?' mused Jonathan.

'I know!' Flavia said, after a moment's thought. 'We'll all hide, and wait for him to go back into the town. When he does, you follow him, Jonathan. Try to find out who he is and where he lives. Nubia and I will go back to the little tomb and look for clues there. Then we'll meet back at my house. All right?'

'Yes, that sounds like a good idea. Let's wait beside that tomb in the shade . . .'

The three of them sat on a soft layer of dust and pine needles, and rested their backs against the shady wall of a large, decrepit tomb. Fragrant dill and thyme bushes screened them from the road, but they could see anyone who came along. For a long time no one passed. The only sound was the slow creaking of the cicadas and Scuto's steady, rhythmic panting.

Flavia gazed at the tombs around them. They were like small houses, with doors, so that new urns could be added. Some had inscriptions above the doors, others had pictures painted on their outer walls, like the two faded gladiators shown fighting on a tomb near the road.

Flavia's own family had a tomb further down the road, for the Gemini family had now been in Ostia for three generations. She often went there with her father to honour her mother and tiny twin brothers.

Half buried amphoras marked the graves of

poorer people. Wine could be poured into their necks to refresh the ashes of the dead below.

Presently an old man leading a tiny donkey passed slowly down the road towards the town. He had loaded the little beast high with firewood. They could hear him singing snatches of a song and talking to himself. Then he was gone and the road was empty again.

'I don't think he's coming this way,' Flavia whispered to Jonathan at last. 'Unless we've missed him . . .'

'No, we haven't missed him. Wait here. I'll see if he is still at the tomb . . .'

He crept off but a few minutes later he stood before them.

'He's gone,' said Jonathan. 'But you must come and look at the tomb. Come quickly!'

'To the gods of the underworld,' Flavia read. 'Sacred to the memory of my poor Avita, eight years old . . .'

The three of them – and Scuto – stood before the little tomb while Flavia read out the Latin inscription painted over the tiny door.

'There's a picture on this side,' said Jonathan. They all moved round to the side of the tomb. Someone had painted a fresco of a little girl lying on a funeral couch surrounded by mourners. The colours looked strangely bright and cheerful.

'Little girl,' said Nubia sadly.

'Yes,' said Flavia softly. 'Probably his daughter. But where did he go? The only way back is along the road.'

'Unless . . .' said Jonathan. 'Unless *his* house backs onto the graveyard like ours.'

'But that would mean he lived on our street,' said Flavia.

'I wonder how we could find out,' mused Jonathan, nibbling a stalk of dried grass.

'I know just the person to ask!' cried Flavia.

They stood in Flavia's kitchen, munching grapes and sipping cool water from ceramic cups. Scuto was drinking long and deeply from his water bowl.

Alma bent over the kitchen hearth, stirring a pan of chicken barley soup and nodding her head.

'Yes, I remember something about a little girl. Her father was a sailor. They lived just up our street. The father adored the girl. Hated to be away from her. That's right, the girl's name was Avita. Avita Procula. And his name was Publius. Publius Avitus Proculus. Came back from a voyage a week or two ago to find she'd died.'

Alma reached up and took a pinch of rosemary from a dried bundle which hung from the ceiling.

'She lived just up the road?' asked Jonathan.

'Yes,' said Alma, crumbling the herb into the soup, 'the house right on the bend.'

'How did Avita die?' asked Flavia. 'Do you know?'

'Oh my, yes,' sighed Alma as she resumed stirring. 'But I never mentioned it to you, dear. I didn't want to give you nightmares . . .'

They all looked at Alma. She stopped stirring for a moment and faced them gravely. 'She died horribly, in great pain, of hydrophobia.' And when they continued to stare at her blankly, she explained in a whisper, 'A mad dog bit her!'

'Hydrophobia,' said Mordecai, 'is a terrible disease.' He was leaning over the marble-topped table in his study, examining medical scrolls.

'The word "hydrophobia" means "a fear of water". People suffering from hydrophobia are terrified of water, even of their own saliva.'

Jonathan, standing behind his father, allowed some spittle to bubble out of his mouth, looked down at it and opened his eyes wide in mock horror. Flavia and Nubia tried not to giggle. Mordecai went on:

'Victims also lose their appetite – '

Jonathan pretended to refuse an imaginary plate.

' – suffer hallucinations '

Jonathan opened his eyes wide again and screamed silently, brushing wildly at imaginary insects crawling on his arms. Flavia bit her lip to stop from laughing. Nubia covered her mouth with her hand.

' – and eventually become paralysed.'

Jonathan clapped his arms to his sides, went stiff as a plank and crossed his eyes. The girls, unable to contain themselves any longer, burst out laughing. Mordecai glanced up at them briefly.

'Jonathan, please,' he said without looking round, 'it's not a laughing matter.' He read on. 'The disease is also known as rabies, which means "a raging". Hmmmn. Let's see what Pliny has to say – I have his new volume here somewhere – '

'Who is Pliny?' asked Flavia.

'He's the admiral of the Roman fleet and a brilliant historian,' said Mordecai as he shuffled through the scrolls on the table. 'He's just written a superb natural history in thirty-seven volumes . . . Lives just down the coast from here . . . Ah!'

Jonathan's father held a scroll to the lamp, for it was nearly dusk and the light was fading quickly.

'Yes! Here's what Pliny says about rabies: "greatest danger of humans catching it when the dog-star is shining" – that's now – "it causes fatal hydrophobia . . . to prevent a dog from catching this disease, mix chicken dung in its food."'

Jonathan screwed up his face and stuck his tongue out.

Mordecai smiled indulgently at their laughter, then suddenly hissed at them to be quiet.

They all heard a strangled cry and the sound of barking.

'They're in the graveyard again,' cried Mordecai between clenched teeth, 'but this time I'm ready.'

The doctor hurried out of the study and ran upstairs, almost tripping on his long robe. Jonathan, Flavia and Nubia followed him into a narrow bedroom with one small window. Under the window a small pile of stones lay on an octagonal table, and next to them a bow and arrow. Mordecai pushed his head out and they heard him grunt.

'There they are!' He reached for the bow and arrow and aimed it through the window.

Jonathan and Flavia jostled to see, but the window was too small. Mordecai was blocking their view.

'Quickly!' cried Jonathan. 'The other bedroom has a window. Follow me!'

SCROLL VIII

The girls followed Jonathan into a second narrow bedroom with bright, mustard-yellow walls. They ran to the window and Jonathan yanked out a wooden lattice-work screen that fitted into its frame. Peering through, they were just in time to see Mordecai's arrow fly into the midst of the pack of dogs which surrounded a tall umbrella pine.

The arrow missed.

The dogs swarmed around the tree, barking loudly and gazing up into it.

'Use your sling,' Flavia urged Jonathan.

'I can't. There's not enough room in here to swing it. I need to be outside.'

Their three faces crowded into the tiny window frame.

'What are they barking at?' asked Jonathan.

'There's something up that tree.'

'Yes,' agreed Jonathan. 'There's something on the other side, clinging on – ' It was difficult to see in the fading light.

'I can see hands. Or maybe paws,' said Flavia.

'Boy,' said Nubia.

'No, it can't be a boy. Look how fast it's climbing now,' cried Jonathan.

'It must be a monkey,' gasped Flavia.

The dogs had stopped barking and were watching the climber with interest, too.

Suddenly the creature moved round the trunk and they could all see its silhouette against the yellow sky of dusk. The creature was not a monkey, but a boy no more than eight years old.

As they watched in amazement, he shouted incoherently down at the dogs: not a scream of fear, but a mocking taunt. This enraged the dogs, who began to bark furiously again.

Another arrow whizzed down from the window. This one found its mark. One of the dogs yelped, leapt into the air, then fell back with a shaft in his gut. The others sniffed at him and, when a second arrow struck the leader, they ran off into the woods. Two dogs with arrows in them lay writhing on the ground. High up in the tree, the small boy clung to the trunk.

'Let's help the boy,' cried Jonathan, and ran downstairs with the girls close behind him.

Mordecai followed them down the stairs.

'Wait!' he cried. 'Don't go out! The dogs aren't dead yet. They may still be dangerous.'

'But we have to help the boy,' protested Jonathan.

'Yes, I know,' his father reassured him, as they

66

reached the bottom of the stairs. 'That's why I brought this . . .'

They all looked at the object Mordecai held in his hand. It was a large, curved sword. The blade was polished to mirror brightness and its edge was sharp as a razor.

The back of the house had no windows at ground level, so the three of them ran back upstairs to the yellow bedroom in order to watch. In the twilight, they saw Jonathan's father emerge cautiously from the back door beneath them. The white oval of his turban gleamed in the dusk. Below it they could see his blue shoulders and the flash of the sword.

He moved slowly towards the pine tree, occasionally glancing up at the boy, but keeping a closer eye on the wounded dogs. The leader lay panting quietly, pinned to the ground by an arrow in his leg. The other – a bitch – writhed in agony with an arrow in her belly. The blade flashed as Mordecai cut the she-dog's throat with a single stroke, putting her out of her misery.

But his action caused the leader to twist with alarm, and in doing so the huge black mastiff freed himself from the ground. The wounded beast faced Mordecai and crouched. His lip curled back to reveal sharp, pale fangs dripping with saliva. The broken shaft protruded from his hind leg.

Mordecai murmured something soothing, though

they could not make out the words, but the wounded hound was not pacified.

With an ugly snarl, he leapt directly at Mordecai's face.

Jonathan's father reacted by instinct. The bloody sword flashed again and the dog's head and body fell in two separate places.

For a moment, no one moved. Then Flavia and her friends raced downstairs and out of the back door.

When they reached Mordecai, he was standing in the same spot, looking down at the two dead dogs and trembling.

'Let me have the sword, father,' said Jonathan quietly.

Mordecai shook his head emphatically. 'No! If these dogs are rabid, even the blood from the sword might be dangerous.' He moved over to a clump of horse-grass and began wiping the blade clean.

Flavia felt a tug at her arm. Nubia was pointing up at the tree. The boy, instead of coming down and thanking them for saving his life, was shimmying higher up the tree.

'Come down,' called Flavia, 'the dogs are dead. It's safe – '

'They can't hurt you now,' Jonathan added.

But the boy had reached the larger limbs and was inching his way along one. His bare feet gripped the branch almost as tightly as his hands. They watched in fascination as he slowly stood up on it, remained still for a moment and then leapt six feet towards another umbrella pine nearby. He caught hold of a branch with one arm, but it was a small one and began to bend alarmingly. They gasped but the boy had already moved on, using his momentum, and swung to the next branch.

There was an even larger gap between the tree he was in and the next one, which led to the woods beyond.

'He'll never make it,' gasped Flavia in horror, as the boy swung from the pine branch, preparing to jump.

'He just might,' breathed Jonathan.

The boy leapt.

He seemed suspended in air for a moment and the four faces watching him seemed frozen, too.

Then, impossibly, he had grasped one of the pine's outermost branches and was swinging for the next, sturdier limb. But as he swung forward they all heard an ominous crack. The branch – and the boy with it – plummeted to the earth below.

'It's a miracle, but it seems no bones are broken,' murmured Mordecai as he examined the boy. 'Jonathan, could you bring the lamp-stand a bit nearer?'

They were all standing round the boy, who lay on a couch in the mustard-yellow bedroom. The boy's eyes were closed and his face was very pale, but he was breathing. Jonathan pulled a standing lamp closer to the bed, carefully, so that the hot oil wouldn't spill.

The light now shone full on the boy's face, and they could see he was exceedingly grubby. Smears of dirt streaked his face and his tangled hair was full of dust and twigs. His tattered tunic smelled curiously of sour wine and pine resin.

Abruptly the boy opened his eyes. They glittered sea-green in the lamplight and for a moment they registered fear. But only for a moment. Then they grew alert and wary.

'Peace be with you,' said Mordecai with a little bow, and added, 'every stranger is an uninvited guest.'

The boy started to rise but Mordecai pushed him gently back against the striped cushions piled on his bed.

'Careful, my boy,' he said softly. 'You've taken a nasty fall. It's a miracle you've no broken bones.'

The boy settled back on the pillows and looked round at them, almost as if judging his chances of escape.

'Jonathan, the bread please . . .' said Mordecai.

Jonathan handed his father a plate with a flat, round loaf of bread on it. Mordecai tore a piece from the loaf and handed it to the boy.

The boy didn't hesitate. He reached a hand out

from under the covers, took the piece of bread, sniffed it quickly and swallowed it almost whole. Flavia noticed that his fingernails were cracked and filthy.

Mordecai set the plate carefully on the couch. The boy took another hunk of bread and devoured it. He ate like a dog, chomping once or twice with his molars and then throwing his head back and swallowing the half-chewed bread in one gulp. Between bites he looked constantly round at them: warily, suspiciously, as if at any moment one of them might suddenly lunge forward to steal his food.

When he had finished the loaf, and drained a beaker of cold water, he wiped his mouth with his bare arm and pushed back the cover as if to go.

'No, no,' Mordecai said gently, pressing him back on the bed. 'You can't leave now. It's already dark outside. Let me get word to your family that you are all right. What is your name, and where do you live?'

The boy looked at him silently, his mouth firmly closed.

'We have shared bread together,' explained Mordecai solemnly. 'You are now under our protection. Please tell us your name.' He smiled encouragingly.

The boy said nothing.

'He doesn't understand us,' said Jonathan.

The boy shot him a furious look.

'Oh, but I think he does,' said Mordecai. 'Young man,' he said gently, 'please open your mouth for me.'

The boy glared at him.

'Please,' said Mordecai softly.

The boy opened his mouth slowly. Mordecai carefully held the boy's chin between thumb and forefinger and lowered it even more. Then he looked into the boy's mouth.

After a moment he closed it again and looked gravely at the three of them.

'He understands well enough,' said the doctor, 'but he is unable to reply. You see, someone has cut out his tongue.'

SCROLL IX

There was a stunned silence as they looked in horror at the boy. He glared defiantly back at them and Flavia saw angry tears fill his eyes. She realised his pride must be injured, and thought quickly.

'I've seen you near the forum, haven't I?' she asked in a conversational tone. 'You often sit by the junk man's stall . . .' She didn't add that she had seen him begging.

The boy looked at her suspiciously for a moment and then gave a small nod. Jonathan followed Flavia's lead.

'How did you learn to climb trees so well?' he asked. 'I've never seen anything like it. Could you teach me?'

The beggar-boy looked pleased, in spite of himself, and shrugged.

Then Nubia spoke:

'What name?' she asked and then corrected herself: 'What your name?'

The others looked at her in horror. Didn't she realise the boy couldn't speak to tell his name?

The boy looked at Nubia for a moment and then growled and snarled like a fierce dog.

'Sorry!' Flavia apologised to the boy.

'We didn't mean to upset you,' added Jonathan hastily.

'Dog?' said Nubia.

Ignoring Flavia and Jonathan, the boy beckoned Nubia on with one hand: she understood what he was trying to say.

'Lion?' she asked.

The boy shook his head, but his gleaming eyes urged her on.

Flavia and Jonathan finally caught on.

'Tiger?' asked Flavia. 'Is Tiger your name?'

The boy shook his head.

'Horse?' suggested Jonathan. The boy looked at him, rolled his eyes heavenward and snarled again, curling his lip back from his teeth.

'Oh, I know!' cried Flavia. 'Wolf!'

The boy gave an emphatic nod of assent.

'Lupus? Is that your name?' asked Flavia. The boy nodded again, folded his arms and sat back on the cushions.

Nubia turned to Flavia.

'What is Lupus?'

'Wolf,' said Flavia, 'like a fierce wild dog.' Then she remembered the word in Greek: 'Lykos!'

'Ah! Lupus!' said Nubia, and gave the boy a

radiant smile. The boy raised his eyebrows questioningly, and pointed back at them.

'I'm Flavia.'

'Jonathan.'

'My name is Nubia,' said the slave-girl. And automatically added, 'How may I please you?'

Lupus dropped his jaw at her in mock astonishment, and the others burst out laughing, even Nubia.

After another hour of questioning, with much nodding and shaking of Lupus's head, they had discovered several facts about him.

Lupus was an orphan. He had no family. He had no home. He spent much of his day searching in the rubbish tips behind the tombs. The junk man occasionally gave him small coins for what he found. With those coins, together with any he received from begging, he bought food. During the summer, when the nights were warm, he slept outside, often among the tombs. In the winter, when it was cold or damp, he slept beside the furnace of the Baths of Thetis. He thought he was about eight years old, but did not know for certain.

None of them dared to ask how he had lost his tongue.

Throughout their exchange, Mordecai had been sitting quietly in a shadowy corner, watching and listening. They had almost forgotten his presence, and when he stood up and came into the circle of lamplight, Flavia jumped.

'Children, it is well past sundown,' he gently reminded them, 'and time for you all to go to bed. Flavia, you and Nubia should go home now, or your nurse will worry. Lupus, you are welcome to spend the night here. Would you like that?'

Lupus considered this proposal for a moment and then nodded.

'Good,' smiled Mordecai.

He pinched out all but one of the wicks on the lamp stand and left the room. Jonathan and Nubia said goodnight to Lupus and went out. Flavia trailed behind on purpose, and as she reached the door, she turned and whispered to the boy:

'Lupus, Jonathan's dog was beheaded this morning. We are trying to find out who killed it. Will you help us solve the mystery?'

Lupus's green eyes glinted in the dim lamplight and she saw him nod.

'See you in the morning then,' said Flavia.

'We're just finishing our breakfast,' said Jonathan the next morning as he led Flavia and Nubia through the atrium and corridor towards the garden.

'Miriam's still at my cousin's house and father went to the forum early to report the crime to the magistrates, and also to tell them about the pack of wild dogs. He says soldiers will probably deal with them. Father told us not to go anywhere until he comes back,' Jonathan added as they stepped into the garden.

It was only an hour after dawn and the garden was still in shadow, though the sky above was clear blue. Lupus was sitting cross-legged on a faded red and blue carpet spread on the garden path. Although the low table before him was loaded with food, he wasn't eating. He was sipping a thick, creamy liquid from a clay beaker.

'It's buttermilk,' explained Jonathan. 'He had some bread and honey, but this is easier for him to eat.'

'Good morning, Lupus,' said Flavia. 'Are you feeling better this morning?' The mute boy greeted Flavia and Nubia with a half smile and nodded. Jonathan and the girls sat around the table on the carpet.

Flavia pulled a wax tablet and stylus from her belt. 'Let's make a plan for today. Jonathan, have you told Lupus everything?'

'Yes,' nodded Jonathan. 'Everything I could remember. How we all went to the harbour with you, leaving Bobas here alone and how we found him when we got back . . .' His voice caught and Flavia asked quickly,

'How do you think the killer got in?'

'Father rarely locks the door,' Jonathan admitted.

'We have no door-slave and in our old community, no one ever locked their doors.' He paused and added softly, 'We'll never make that mistake again.'

'Who lives on the other side of this house, Jonathan?'

'A banker and his family, I think, but they shut it up last week and went to Herculaneum for the summer.'

'Hmmm.' Flavia made a few notes on her wax tablet. 'No one *heard* anything, no-one *saw* anything – apart from Libertus – and nothing was stolen . . .'

'The dice!' cried Jonathan. 'I forgot about the dice!'

He fished in the pouch tied to his belt and showed Lupus the quartz dice. Lupus blew on it, rolled it on the carpet and scowled as it came up one.

'The dog throw,' observed Flavia absently, and then: 'Wait! When you throw a one it's called the dog throw! It's the worst score. Do you think it means something?'

Jonathan shrugged, and Lupus scratched his head.

'Probably not . . .' Flavia chewed the end of her stylus. 'I think the killer was the man crying beside the tomb,' she said finally. 'He hates dogs and he fits Libertus's description. Did you tell Lupus what the man looked like?'

Jonathan started to reply, but suddenly Lupus grabbed Flavia's wax tablet and stylus and rubbed out her notes with his thumb.

'Hey!' said Flavia in protest.

Lupus ignored her and began to make a few quick marks on the tablet. He grinned with delight as the tip of the ivory stylus pushed back the soft beeswax to reveal blackened wood beneath. Flavia was about to snatch it back when she saw that he was drawing something. After a moment, the boy held it up for them to see.

With confident black lines etched in the yellow wax, Lupus had drawn a man. The portrait was simple but clear: a square face, clean-shaven, short hair brushed forward and heavy eyebrows that met above his nose.

'That's him!' exclaimed Flavia with a squeal of excitement. 'That's the man we saw at the tomb!'

SCROLL X

'That's amazing!' breathed Jonathan, admiring Lupus's sketch of the man. 'Who taught you to draw?'

Lupus pushed out his lower lip and shrugged, as if to say it was not difficult.

'Do you know this man?' asked Flavia.

Lupus shook his head.

'Then how could you draw him?'

Lupus jerked his thumb back towards the grave-yard. Then he mimicked someone weeping.

'You've seen him crying at his daughter's grave, too!'

Lupus nodded.

'When?' asked Jonathan.

Lupus thought for a moment, flicked up three fingers, then four.

'Four different times?'

He nodded.

'My old nurse Alma told us that his name was Publius Avitus Proculus,' Flavia said to Lupus. 'He's a sailor and he lives further up this street.'

'Why kill dog?' asked Nubia suddenly.

'He hates all dogs because his daughter was killed by one,' explained Jonathan. 'Hates dogs. Thinks dogs bad.'

'No, wait,' said Flavia. 'Nubia's right. Why *did* he kill Bobas? Bobas was a tame dog, not a wild one. And he was shut up here in the house.'

'Perhaps Bobas looked like the dog who bit his daughter,' suggested Jonathan. 'Or maybe he was passing by, and heard Bobas bark and became mad with grief and killed him . . .'

'Maybe . . .' said Flavia. 'Still, we've got to be sure it was him, before we accuse him of such a crime . . .' They were all silent for a few moments.

'I know!' cried Flavia, suddenly. 'Let's show your drawing to Libertus across the street, and see if he thinks it's the same man he saw running away.'

'Good idea,' agreed Jonathan, and then his face fell. 'But my father told me to stay inside until he got back. Lupus, too. And I have to do my chores.'

'Then Nubia and I will go!' announced Flavia, and seeing Jonathan's disappointed face, she added, 'Don't worry. We'll come straight back.'

Flavia hesitated for a moment before Cordius's house and then rapped on the door. The knocker was a fat bronze dolphin whose nose banged loudly on a bronze scallop shell.

'Knocker,' said Flavia to Nubia automatically, as

they waited for a reply. Then: 'Dolphin. Shell. Green. Green door. Dog barking. Peephole. Opening . . .

'Hello!' she said politely to the beady eyes that appeared in the tiny window. 'I know your master is away, but may we speak to Libertus please?' The eyes regarded her suspiciously.

'My father is your master's client,' added Flavia.

After a moment, the sliding door of the peephole shut and they heard the grate of the bolt sliding back. An extremely thin slave with a sour face opened the door.

Straining against a leash wrapped round his hand was a large red hound who snarled and bared his teeth at them.

Flavia shrank back in alarm, but Nubia slowly extended the back of her hand to the dog and spoke softly in her own language. Immediately, the dog stopped snarling and sniffed her hand. Then he licked it.

The doorkeeper cursed the dog under his breath, and beckoned the girls in. Flavia hesitated on the threshold. On the floor was a mosaic. Tiny pieces of coloured clay and stone showed a fierce black dog against a red background. The mosaic dog was straining against his lead and baring sharp teeth, and below him were the words CAVE CANEM: 'Beware of the dog!'

'I certainly will!' muttered Flavia under her breath.

'Wait here,' grumbled the sour-faced porter, and went off with his dog to find Libertus.

While they waited in the atrium, Flavia and Nubia looked around in wonder. Flavia had never been in Cordius's house before. It was the home of a very wealthy man: at least three times as big as hers.

The atrium had a beautiful floor of black and white marble, and in its middle – under the open skylight – a fountain bubbled in a gold-tiled impluvium. On the walls around them were frescoes depicting scenes from the travels of Aeneas, the legendary hero who founded Rome.

'Look,' pointed Nubia. 'Dog with three heads.'

Flavia gazed in delight at the pictures on the wall. 'Yes, it's Cerberus. Cerberus. He is very fierce. He's the hound who guards the gates of the underworld. Land of dead people.'

'Cerberus,' said Nubia in wonder and walked over to the wall. Flavia followed her and they both examined the three-headed hound opening all his mouths at a startled Aeneas. Behind Aeneas, a woman held out her hand to the dog.

'I don't remember that part of the *Aeneid*,' murmured Flavia to herself.

'Book six,' said a man's voice behind them, and they both started guiltily. It was Libertus, but he did not seem angry. His dark blue eyes sparkled as he quoted: ' "Huge Cerberus makes the caves of the underworld echo with his three-throated barking . . ." '

Libertus pointed.

'That's the scene where Aeneas's guide gives the hellhound a drugged biscuit, so that he can pass by . . .'

Libertus nodded at the frescoes with approval. 'They're beautiful, aren't they?' he said.

'Very beautiful,' agreed Flavia.

'Come through to the garden,' he said with a smile. 'As you know, Cordius is away, and in his absence I am the master of his house.'

He led them out of the atrium and down some steps into a beautiful garden as big as Flavia's entire house. At its centre was a large ornamental pool with two bronze dolphins spouting water at each other. Six laurel trees, trimmed into perfect balls, had been planted on either side of the pool, and at one end stood an elegant palm tree, its top half lit gold-green by the early morning sun.

Flavia could see mosaic patterns on the garden paths and bronze statues half hidden in the fragrant shrubbery. She heard the snip of a gardener's shears and then noticed another slave sweeping the peristyle – the columned walkway that surrounded the garden. There was not a leaf out of place and even the dew on the mimosa seemed to sparkle like diamonds.

'Please sit.' Libertus gestured to a cedarwood couch with orange linen cushions. Taking a seat on a similar couch opposite the girls, he leaned forward, elbows on knees, and smiled.

'How may I help you, Flavia Gemina?'

'Remember we told you yesterday that Jonathan's dog was killed?'

'Yes,' he replied gravely and a frown creased his smooth forehead, 'a terrible matter.'

'And you saw a man running?'

'Yes. Carrying a leather bag . . .'

'Well – is this the man you saw?' Flavia pulled the wax tablet from her belt and showed it to him.

Libertus took the tablet from her and examined it carefully.

'Yes,' he said slowly, 'clean-shaven, hair combed forward, and those heavy eyebrows – yes!' He nodded. 'I remember the eyebrows, how they met over his eyes. And I think he was wearing a pale tunic.'

'Pale yellow?'

'It *was* pale yellow, now that you mention it. Yes! I'm certain this is the man I saw running down the street yesterday!'

The girls had just told Jonathan and Lupus their exciting news about the running man when they heard a knock on the door and Mordecai's voice calling his son.

'We really must get a new watchdog,' sighed Mordecai as they let him in. 'I do miss Bobas,' he added sadly.

Jonathan had cleared away the breakfast things and now he brought his father a cup of mint tea. They all sat on the carpet in a sunlit corner of the garden.

Mordecai was wearing a Roman-style tunic and mantle, presumably to impress the city officials, and for the first time Flavia saw him without his turban. His hair was black, streaked with grey, and quite long. He had tied it all back, including the distinctive locks which usually fell in front of his ears.

'The magistrates have received other complaints about the wild dogs and they assured me that they have men out looking for them even now. They promised they would bury the dogs I killed last night. As for the crime of Bobas's killing, it's not so simple. They're reluctant to get involved.'

Mordecai sipped his mint tea reflectively.

'I have an appointment to see an official later this morning and then I must visit some patients, so I may be out all day. Flavia, may Jonathan and Lupus stay at your house? I don't want to leave them here alone . . .'

'Of course,' said Flavia. 'They'll be perfectly safe at our house.'

'I've locked our door,' said Mordecai to the four of

them a short time later. They were standing on the hot pavement outside Flavia's house.

'Here's the key, Jonathan. Keep it at Flavia's, and only use it if you need to get in urgently. With any luck I'll be back shortly after midday, but who knows? With city officials, anything is possible. Now promise me you won't get into trouble and that you won't go far.'

'I promise that we won't even leave this street, father,' said Jonathan earnestly.

'Very well,' smiled Mordecai. 'Peace be with you, my children.'

'Peace be with you,' they answered, and watched him hurry up the road.

As soon as he turned the corner by the green fountain, Flavia turned to Jonathan.

'We promised not leave our street,' she said, 'but Avitus's house is on this street and I've just thought of a brilliant plan for getting in!'

SCROLL XI

'Avitus might recognise the three of us from the graveyard yesterday,' Flavia began, 'but if I pinned my hair up and put on a nice stola, and went with Lupus, I don't think he'd recognise me.'

The four of them were sitting on the marble bench in Flavia's garden while she told them her plan to find out more about Avitus, the man they had seen weeping in the graveyard.

'A disguise!' cried Jonathan. 'What a good idea!'

Flavia explained the rest of her plan and the others agreed it was a clever one.

'There's only one problem,' he pointed out. 'For your plan to work, we'll have to clean up Lupus. I mean *really* clean him up . . .'

They all looked at Lupus.

'You're right,' agreed Flavia. 'It'll take a little extra time, but it has to be done. You'll have to take him, Jonathan, and Caudex can go with you.' She turned to Lupus.

'I know you've slept outside the Baths of Thetis,' she said with a grin, 'but have you ever been *inside* them?'

A few hours later, at mid-day, Flavia was reading book six of the *Aeneid* to Nubia. Suddenly Scuto, curled up at their feet, lifted his head and uttered a bark, and shortly afterwards they heard a knock at the front door.

'We'll get it, Alma!' Flavia called, and hastily put down the scroll. 'They're back!' she exulted. 'Oh, I can't wait to see this!'

The girls hurried to the door. Scuto sensed their excitement and ran barking after them, his claws skittering on the marble floor.

Flavia slid back the bolt and threw open the door to reveal Caudex and the two boys. All three wore large grins.

'Lupus!' cried Flavia. 'You're clean! Your skin is three shades lighter! And they've cut your hair!'

'Shaved it more like!' said Jonathan, patting Lupus's fuzzy stubble. 'His head was crawling with nits!'

'Even that old tunic looks cleaner,' marvelled Flavia.

'They cleaned and pressed our clothes while we were in the baths,' said Jonathan, stepping into the atrium. 'Show them your hands, Lupus!'

Lupus held out his hands reluctantly as he followed Jonathan in. They were almost spotless and the nails neatly manicured. Nubia commented shyly,

'Smell nice!'

Scuto sniffed at Lupus's foot and then sneezed.

Caudex, who smelled strongly of rose oil, closed the door behind them and took up his usual post.

'I don't think Lupus liked the steam room much,' said Jonathan over his shoulder, 'but I couldn't get him out of the pool. He's a brilliant swimmer and he was as happy as a newt in a puddle. Weren't you, Lupus?'

Lupus nodded as they went into the garden.

'You're not limping any more!' cried Flavia.

'We both had a long massage,' said Jonathan. 'I thought it might ease his aches and bruises.'

'And did it?' Flavia asked Lupus.

For a reply, the beggar-boy nodded again.

'Hmmmn,' said Flavia. 'The only thing he needs now are sandals. He can't go in bare feet!'

'I have some at home. I outgrew them last year, but they're still in good condition . . .' suggested Jonathan.

'You and Lupus take the key and get them,' said Flavia, 'while I change into a different person, too!'

A girl and a boy stood outside a house with a red door at the bend of Green Fountain Street. The girl had clear grey eyes and wore a white stola. Her light brown hair was neatly coiled on top of her head, though one or two strands had already escaped. The boy had green eyes and very short brown hair. His tunic was faded but clean. Both wore bullas around their necks, marking them out as freeborn.

The girl knocked again. Presently, an old man opened the red door and after a moment they all disappeared inside.

Meanwhile, behind the same house in the grave-yard, another boy and girl were climbing a tall poplar tree. The girl moved up quietly and fluidly, as if she had climbed trees all her life. She was beautiful, with very short black hair, dark brown skin and golden eyes. Among the dark leaves of the poplar, she was almost invisible. The boy who followed her had dark, curly hair, a strong, straight nose and eyes so dark they were almost black. Unlike the girl, he was not a graceful climber: he kept getting poked in the eye with twigs and leaves. And under his breath he uttered words a polite Roman boy should not even have known.

Flavia looked around the atrium. It had originally been the same size as the one in her house, but flimsy rooms had been constructed on either side, making it a narrow, dark corridor. An entire family seemed to occupy the atrium. She could hear a child singing tunelessly behind one of the curtained door-ways, and a woman was washing nappies in the impluvium. Beside her squatted two runny-nosed toddlers, intent on a game they were playing with seed-pods and pine cones.

'Avitus and his wife have the balcony rooms,' mumbled the toothless old man. 'Go through the garden and up the stairs . . .' He didn't wait for a reply, but shuffled back to his cubicle and disappeared behind the curtain.

The woman washing clothes nodded at them as they squeezed by and Flavia murmured a polite greeting. Damp laundry hung from a washing line beneath the skylight, blocking off what little sunshine managed to enter the dismal room. A faint odour of stale sweat and frying onions hung in the air.

Flavia tugged Lupus's hand and they moved hesitantly down the corridor into what should have been the garden. Here too, old rooms had been enlarged and new rooms built, so that the garden had shrunk to a few paving stones with weeds pushing between them. A wizened vine struggled up a rickety trellis towards what little light there was.

It was hotter in the garden than in the atrium. The family who occupied this part of the house had left the curtains of their cubicles open to catch any breeze. It was still siesta time and Flavia glimpsed suspicious eyes watching her from low beds in the dim rooms.

As she and Lupus started up the stairs a young woman in a black stola appeared on the balcony above them. She had a long nose and small mouth, and large, moist brown eyes.

'Have you come to see me?' The woman called down.

'We've come to see if Avita can play,' said Flavia in her little-girl voice. 'My name is um . . . Helena, and this is my brother Lucius. We have just returned from a voyage.'

'Oh!' cried the woman, and then said, 'You'd better come up.'

She met them at the top of the stairs and led them into a small, stuffy room with a low couch against one wall and a table against the other. A few flies buzzed round the remains of a meal on the table. The woman in black perched on a stool and invited the two of them to sit on the couch. Flavia noticed that some of the plaster was missing from the ceiling and one or two cracks snaked along the walls.

'My name is Julia Firma,' said the woman. 'I have some very sad news. My daughter died several weeks ago.'

Lupus burst into tears, quite convincingly, Flavia thought. She pretended to pat him consolingly. Then she said to Julia, 'But Avita always seemed so healthy.'

'I'm afraid she was bitten by a rabid dog. '

'Oh how awful!' cried Flavia. 'How did it happen?'

'It's so crowded here, as you can see.' Avita's mother waved vaguely towards the garden. 'My daughter loved to play in the graveyard among the trees and I never thought . . .'

Her voice trailed off and she swatted absently at a fly. 'One day she came home complaining of a dog bite. She was very brave. She cried a little but it was not deep, so I merely put ointment on it and didn't think about it again.' The woman closed her eyes for a moment and then continued.

'After a few days, we suspected something was wrong. First, Avita lost her appetite and then she began to be terrified of the sight of water. She even refused to drink. Finally she began to see things that weren't there. The end, when it came, was peaceful.'

Julia looked down and brushed some plaster dust from her dark stola.

'The tragedy was that her father was away on a voyage when it happened. Avita was our only surviving child and when my husband returned and discovered that we had lost her, he was inconsolable. He doesn't share my faith,' she added quietly.

'Your faith?' asked Flavia.

'I believe that after we die, we will go to a place more wonderful than we can imagine. Not the cold, dark underworld, but a sunny garden – a paradise. I trust Avita is there now. She was also a believer.' Julia Firma gazed at the faded plaster wall with a smile, as if she could see through it to a world beyond. Lupus and Flavia exchanged glances.

'Would you children like to see her room?' Avita's mother asked suddenly.

'Yes, please.' Flavia nodded politely, remembering to use her little-girl voice.

Julia Firma rose and led them next door into a tiny bedroom. A small window looked out onto the graveyard and the walls were decorated with faded frescoes of trees, shrubs and birds.

'She loved this room,' sighed Julia, and looked around with a sad smile. 'She used to tell me paradise would be like this.'

A narrow bed occupied most of the cubicle, which was tiny but spotlessly clean. At the head of the sleeping couch was a low table with Avita's possessions still laid out: a clay lamp, a few tiny glass bottles, a bronze mirror, and a wooden comb. On the bed lay a small painting of the girl.

Flavia and Lupus gazed at the portrait of Avita. Coloured wax had been applied to a flat piece of limewood with such skill that the face painted there seemed about to speak. The girl wore small gold earrings and a bulla round her neck.

The face gazing back at them seemed so cheerful and alert that Flavia's throat tightened painfully: for the first time she really felt the tragedy of the girl's death.

Lupus picked up the portrait to examine it more closely and Flavia gazed out of the window into the graveyard. She couldn't see Jonathan or Nubia anywhere, but as she pushed her face further out, she caught a spicy whiff of grasses and pine needles. She breathed the scent of life gratefully and then turned back to look for clues on the table.

The clay oil-lamp caught her eye. Its design was one she had never seen before. On its top – where most lamps had a cupid or a leaf – was a beardless man with a lamb across his shoulders.

'The shepherd,' murmured Julia, stepping in from the doorway. 'He has carried my little Avita home, like that lamb.'

'The shepherd?' said Flavia.

'Our God,' Julia replied simply. 'See the Greek letters alpha and omega on the spout? They mean . . .'

But Flavia never heard what she was going to say.

At that moment an angry voice behind them cried, 'What are you doing in my daughter's room? I warned you!'

Lupus whirled round and Flavia dropped the little clay lamp onto the floor. There in the doorway stood Publius Avitus Proculus. And he was very angry.

SCROLL XII

'I told you never to come in here,' shouted Avitus. He was rigid with anger and his heavy eyebrows made him look very fierce. But his anger was directed at his wife, not at Flavia and Lupus.

'But Publius!' Julia protested. 'These children were her friends. I was just showing them – '

'Get out!' Avitus commanded his wife.

For a tense moment they stared at one another.

'No I will not!' Julia finally said. 'She was my daughter, too. You're not the only one who misses her!'

'Yes, but *you'll* see her again one day in paradise, won't you?' There was bitter sarcasm in Avitus's voice.

'That doesn't mean I don't miss her now, Publius . . .' A tear slipped down her cheek. '. . . just as much as you do.'

Suddenly her husband sagged. The anger drained from his face and he began to weep.

'It's my fault she died!' he cried. 'If I had been here . . . I wasn't even here when she . . .'

Julia Firma went to her husband and put her arms

97

round him. 'Of course it wasn't your fault. It wasn't anyone's fault. You must forgive yourself, Publius.'

Avitus and his wife wept in each other's arms and Flavia felt her own eyes prickle with tears. Lupus cleared his throat to attract her attention and made a tiny movement with his head towards the stairs.

Flavia nodded, and the two of them squeezed past the weeping couple and hurried quietly downstairs. They passed through the narrow garden and dark atrium, stepping carefully over the toddlers, and let themselves out.

As the door closed behind them, Flavia shivered and stood silently for a moment in the hot street, soaking up the intense warmth of the afternoon sun.

The next moment they heard the sound of feet pounding the pavement and looked up to see Nubia and Jonathan running towards them.

'Head gone!' said Nubia who reached them first.

And when Jonathan stood before them – wheezing and unable to speak – she said again, 'Dog's head is gone!'

The four friends stood in the graveyard and looked at the bodies of the two dead dogs under the tree. The corpses had already been picked at by crows. Now ants were doing their work, too. Flavia instinctively averted her eyes and then forced herself to look back. There were two bodies, a brown one

98

and a black one, but only one head: the mastiff's big head had disappeared.

'Perhaps a crow carried it off,' Jonathan suggested.

Flavia gave him a sceptical look. 'Too heavy. It's more likely that your father took it to the magistrate for some reason.'

'I don't think so. Remember, he said even the blood might be dangerous.'

'Perhaps one of the dogs from the pack carried it off.'

'Perhaps.' Jonathan sounded doubtful.

Lupus cautiously searched the dry weeds around the leader's headless body. Then he crouched down and sniffed.

'Any clues, Lupus?' Flavia asked him.

He shook his head.

'Better get away from those corpses,' said a deep voice.

The four of them jumped. Behind them two soldiers stood leaning on shovels and perspiring heavily in the heat.

'We're to dispose of them as soon as possible,' said the taller of the two. 'Orders of the magistrate.' He thrust his shovel into the dry ground.

'Did you take the black dog's head?' Flavia asked when she had recovered from her surprise.

'No, sweetheart! Why should we do that?' His shovel sliced into the ground again.

'Well, it's not here and I just wondered – '

'She's right, Rufus!' said the short one, who was leaning on his spade. 'There's a missing head.'

'You'll be missing a head, too, if you don't start helping me dig!'

'What did you find out at Avita's?' whispered Jonathan as they stood in the shade of a pine, watching the soldiers work.

'Nothing much. Her parents both miss her, but her mother believes she's gone to some wonderful garden with a shepherd.'

Jonathan gave Flavia an odd look. She added,

'Avitus came in when we were in her room and got very angry. He does have a bad temper . . .'

'We already know that,' murmured Jonathan, and then added thoughtfully, 'we must find out more about him. If only we could follow him.'

Lupus tugged hopefully at Jonathan's tunic and pointed eagerly at himself.

'Thanks for offering to follow him, Lupus, but I think he'd recognise you now that he's seen you.'

Lupus's response was to bend down, pick up a handful of twigs and dust, and smear them over his face.

'Oh, Lupus!' cried Flavia. 'Just after we got you cleaned up!'

'He's right!' cried Jonathan. 'Everybody knows the beggar-boy at the junk man's stall. And no one ever takes any notice of him. Dressed like a beggar, Lupus is as good as invisible.' He slapped Lupus on the back and said, 'Better take off those sandals and my bulla and put on your own tunic again.'

When Lupus had been restored to his former filthy state, they left him sitting in the shade of a mulberry tree within sight of Avitus's front door. Flavia gave him his last instructions.

'When Avitus comes out of his house – *if* he comes out – follow him at a distance and look for any suspicious behaviour. If he leaves, use this piece of chalk to make an arrow on the tree trunk to show which way you've gone. Here's some bread and cheese in case you get hungry. Better put them out of sight.'

Lupus slipped them into a little cloth pouch tied to the belt of his tunic.

'You're sure you don't mind just sitting here and waiting?' asked Jonathan.

Lupus shook his head.

'We'll try to find out more about Avitus, too,' Flavia told Lupus. 'We'll all meet back at my house an hour before sunset to discuss our findings. Agreed?'

Lupus nodded. Flavia, Nubia and Jonathan set off back down the road. As they passed their house Nubia said to Flavia, 'Take Scuto?'

Flavia hesitated. Someone was killing dogs and she didn't want anything to happen to him. Her father had always told her never to venture into the city without Scuto, but surely if there were three of them they wouldn't come to any danger.

'I think he's safer at home with Caudex and Alma,' she decided.

'Shouldn't you tell them where you're going?' suggested Jonathan.

'If I do, they'll never let us go!' said Flavia. 'Come on!'

Lupus sat under the shade of the mulberry tree and looked up and down the street. It was the hottest part of the day. Most people would be napping in their cool gardens or relaxing at the baths. The street shimmered with heat as Lupus watched the others disappear round the bend in the road.

A flash of movement caught his eye as a slave emptied a chamber pot from an upstairs window. A splash and the squeak of wooden shutters being shut again, and then silence, apart from the chirring of the cicadas.

Lupus thought about Flavia and her friends for a while. Then he thought of all the food he'd eaten in the past few hours.

He usually hated food. He couldn't taste it, it was difficult to chew, and every bite threatened to choke him if he didn't swallow carefully. But when he had been presented with grapes and bread and honey and buttermilk, his body had craved it so badly that he had eaten in spite of the danger.

Now his belly was full and content. He felt sleepy, too. The slow rhythmic creaking of the cicadas in the hot summer afternoon made him feel drowsy. His eyelids grew heavy and almost shut. He shook himself awake angrily.

That was one advantage to being hungry all the time: it gave you an edge, an alertness. His sense of smell was always sharper if he hadn't eaten for a day or two. His eyesight was keener, too.

Was this how ordinary people felt most of the time, full and content and muzzy? He had smeared his face with dust and dirt but under his dirty old tunic his skin felt soft and clean, his muscles loose and relaxed. He could still smell the sandalwood oil they had massaged him with. It made him feel soft and vulnerable. The itching of vermin always used to help him stay alert and awake. But now there were no lice in his clothing and no nits in his hair.

He reached up and stroked his head and felt the soft stubble. It felt nice. How good it would be to live in a beautiful house like Flavia's and always have a full belly and clean clothes and to be able to nap during the hottest part of the afternoon in a cool garden by a splashing fountain. Or go to the baths whenever you wanted and swim in pools of crystal clear water with mosaics of sea nymphs at the bottom, and have all your aches massaged away.

How wonderful never to have to worry about where your next meal would come from. Never to have to worry about people who wanted to hurt you. Never to have to worry about being lonely. Lupus's eyes closed and for a moment he began to slip into the delicious oblivion of sleep.

Suddenly he started awake. Something had moved in the hot, deserted street. The red door was opening. A man closed it behind him and turned to go north towards the Roman Gate. It was Avitus and he was alone.

SCROLL XIII

'Where are you taking us?' Jonathan hesitated as they reached the green fountain that marked the end of their street.

'To the marina forum. The harbourmaster is my father's friend. He might know more about Avitus.'

'But I promised my father we wouldn't leave the street.' Jonathan shifted uneasily on the hot pavement.

'Come on, Jonathan,' Flavia said in her most persuasive voice. 'Don't you want to find out who killed Bobas?'

'Of course I do. But father trusts me.'

'He trusts you to help him,' Flavia said softly. 'It won't take long. I promise.'

Nubia looked from one to the other. After a moment Jonathan said abruptly:

'All right. Let's get this over with.' He set off down Fullers Street at a quick pace, and the girls hurried after him.

Apart from one or two slaves running errands for their masters, the whole town had gone indoors to seek refuge from the heat. Flavia and her friends were damp with sweat by the time they reached the Marina Gate. Through the marble arch, brilliant white against the azure sky, they could see the darker cobalt blue of the sea.

'The harbourmaster's name is Lucius Cartilius Poplicola,' said Flavia as they all paused for a moment in the cool shade beneath the arch. Flavia pointed to the left.

'I think he works there.'

The marina forum was an open square surrounded on three sides by a covered, column-lined walkway.

In the mornings and late afternoons, stalls set up in the shade of this colonnade did brisk business selling select goods fresh off the ships: fish, exotic fruit, jewellery, perfume, wine and fabrics.

Now most of the stalls were closed for the long afternoon lunch. Only one or two remained open. Somewhere a flute warbled and nearby a fishmonger was calling, 'Fresh squid! Last of the catch! Fresh squid!' in a sleepy voice. At the far end of the square stood an imposing brick and marble building.

'His office is in there?' asked Jonathan.

'I think so,' replied Flavia, her confidence faltering. The door was guarded by a soldier on either side.

'Well, come on, then,' said Jonathan, and headed for the building.

As the three friends hurried under the shady

colonnade past mostly empty stalls, the sound of the flute grew louder. Suddenly, Flavia felt Nubia grip her hand.

'Look!' Nubia whispered.

Behind one of the stalls stood a tall, handsome African. His skin was deep brown, like Nubia's, and he had the same neat ears and amber eyes. He was blowing into a little flute made of dark wood.

The three friends stopped before his stall. On a large piece of peacock-blue silk lay flutes of many different shapes, sizes and colours. When the flautist saw them he put down his instrument and smiled with perfect white teeth. He addressed Nubia in a soft, fluid language.

Nubia's face lit up and she replied in the same tongue. As she and the young man conversed, Flavia and Jonathan looked at her in amazement. Speaking her own language, she seemed completely different: confident and proud.

Nubia and the young man spoke together for a few minutes and then the slave-girl pointed to a small flute, like the one he had been playing. The man smiled apologetically and said something to her. Then he turned to Flavia and Jonathan:

'The one she is asking about is made of lotus wood from my country. Very expensive. One gold piece. One hundred sesterces.'

Flavia gasped. One hundred sesterces was a soldier's monthly wage.

'Come on, Nubia,' she said, 'you can come back and talk to him another day soon.'

Nubia followed the others towards the harbour master's office. She only looked back once.

'Avitus?' bawled out the captain of the *Triton* to Flavia and her friends an hour later. 'He wouldn't hurt a fly. Very moody, though. Always writing poetry. About dolphins and waves and sea nymphs. Laughing one minute, crying the next. Doted on that little girl of his, though. I've never seen anyone so affected by the death of a child.'

Flavia, Jonathan and Nubia were standing on one of the small piers of the marina watching a ship called the *Triton* undergo repairs. They hadn't been able to see Poplicola, but an ancient porter in the harbour offices had told them the name of Avitus's ship and even where it was berthed. Captain Alga was halfway up the mast of his ship but his voice was so loud that they could hear him even over the jingle of tackle, the slap of waves against the pier and the shouts and hammering of the sailors.

'Have you seen him recently?' shouted Flavia.

'Avitus?' Captain Alga yelled back. 'No, he's on leave until tomorrow. Then we're off to Sicily again. We've been stuck here for two weeks trying to get our mast refitted. The old one was shattered in a storm. Most amazing storm I've ever experienced. Really thought we were going to Neptune's palace, if you know what I mean. All of us thanking whatever gods we believe in that we're alive and no sooner does he step off the ship than he's greeted with the news of his daughter's death. Told me he wished he had drowned in the storm and had never known what happened to her. Poor little thing – '

The captain would have bellowed on, but Flavia hastily shouted her thanks and led the others back up the pier.

'Well, *he* didn't seem to think Avitus was dangerous,' mused Flavia. 'But Libertus saw Avitus running with a bag, and . . .' Her voice trailed off as she considered the problem.

A fishing boat had just docked and the fishermen were unloading the day's catch. Two lean young men, naked apart from loincloths and as brown as chestnuts, were carrying baskets of gleaming fish down a wobbly boarding plank. One of them nearly slipped and fell, but he regained his balance and leapt lightly onto the pier while the other cursed him good-naturedly.

Nubia stared at the gangplank and shivered. It reminded her of the first time she had been forced to board a ship, at Alexandria. Venalicius had cracked his whip and forced them towards a narrow piece of wood which bridged the land and the boat. The gangplank rose and fell as if it were breathing and Shanakda – a girl from her clan – had screamed hysterically and refused to go up it, alarming all the others. Without warning, Venalicius had furiously unlocked her collar and pushed her into the water, though her hands had still been tied.

Nubia would never forget the sight of bitter seawater filling Shanakda's screaming mouth and silencing her forever. They had all been quiet after that. Quiet and cowed for the whole voyage to Italia.

Nubia shivered again and felt Flavia's arm around her shoulders.

'I know you don't like boats, Nubia,' whispered Flavia. 'We'll go home right now . . .'

But as they turned left and started back towards the Marina Gate, Nubia saw a sight which made her heart pound. Three large men were sauntering straight towards them. Nubia knew them immediately. Their faces appeared often in her nightmares. They were Venalicius's henchmen, from the slave ship.

Nubia stopped short and looked frantically round, squinting against the glare of the sun on the water. The slave ship *Vespa* was berthed in the marina! She would know that hateful black and yellow striped sail anywhere. And there was Venalicius himself, leering at her from the deck with his one good eye.

'Run for your lives!' cried Nubia. She gripped Flavia's arm tightly, 'Venalicius has seen us and sent his men to capture us!'

'What? What about Venalicius?' Flavia frowned at her.

Nubia suddenly realised she had been speaking in her native language. Now she tried to remember the Latin for 'run' but her mind had gone blank.

The men were getting closer. One of them was looking directly at her and smiling an evil smile.

In desperation, Nubia pointed towards the men, and then towards Venalicius.

Flavia saw the slave-dealer watching them from his ship and understood at once.

'Run, Jonathan! Run!' She grabbed his arm and pulled.

They turned and began to run back along the waterfront away from the Marina Gate: Flavia first, then Nubia, then Jonathan.

'Why are we running?' shouted Jonathan, leaping over a rolled up fishnet.

'Venalicius's men are after us!' Flavia dodged a sailor.

'Who's Venalicius?'

'Slave dealer!' shouted Flavia. 'If he catches us, he'll sell us on the far side of the world, where nobody will ever find us.'

She led them round a half-loaded cart, under an unmanned customs stall, and past the building site of the new marina baths.

'Are they still after us?' Flavia called over her shoulder.

'Yes!' gasped Jonathan.

Flavia's ankle started to ache and she realised Jonathan was wheezing. She had to find them some way of escape quickly. The marina piers were on the right. They'd be trapped if they went down one of those. There were some brick warehouses on the left, but again, if they went into one of those there might be no way out. The beach lay ahead of them, but there was no shelter there.

Suddenly Jonathan cried:

'I know where we can hide! Follow me!'

He turned and raced up the narrow alley between the last two warehouses on the waterfront. The alley was narrow and dark. It smelled of urine and vomit and worse. The ground was slippery with rotting fish scales and garbage.

Flavia hoped Jonathan knew what he was doing.

If he didn't, and if Venalicius's men caught them, she knew the three of them would be tied up in the hold of the slave-ship Vespa by that evening.

SCROLL XIV

Slipping from shadow to shadow, Lupus silently followed Avitus to Ropemakers Street. Red brick tenement houses three and four storeys high rose on either side of the street. Their ground floors were all taken up by one-roomed workshops which sold rope, nets, canvas and basketry. These shops were shuttered up, for the shopkeepers had retired to their apartments to rest until the day grew cooler.

Squeezed between two workshops at the end of the street nearest the theatre, was a narrow doorway. A wooden bead curtain hung in this doorway, and above it someone had painted an Egyptian eye. At least a dozen cats, half-starved and half-wild, napped in the bright sun beside the doorway. The timid creatures scattered as Avitus approached this doorway and pushed through the curtain.

Lupus knew almost everyone in this part of town, and he knew the woman who occupied the tiny room behind the bead curtain. She was an Egyptian soothsayer who called herself Hariola.

As quietly as a grass snake, Lupus slipped across the street, closer to the doorway. Then, making himself as small as possible, he sat in the narrow shadow cast by the overhang of one of the shops.

No one would notice him, and even if they did, they would just see a sleepy beggar-boy. He listened as hard as a rabbit, but although he could hear a man's muffled voice and then Hariola's husky croak, he could not make out their words. The voices went silent for a while. Lupus guessed the soothsayer was poking at chicken entrails or staring into a sacred bauble. Presently the woman's voice rang out, it sounded dramatic and false. Then he heard the man replying angrily and now he could hear the words clearly.

'You're lying! You don't know a thing about it!' Avitus shouted.

Abruptly, there was a clatter of beads as Avitus pushed through the curtain. A moment later the wooden beads rattled again and at the same time the sickly-sweet aroma of cheap musk filled Lupus's nostrils: the soothsayer had come out, too.

'Where's my money?' she hissed. 'That's three sesterces you owe me!'

Lupus did not dare put his head round the wall to look. Then he heard Avitus's retreating footsteps and Hariola's rasping voice: 'Unless you offer a sacrifice to the god Anubis, your daughter's spirit will never be at rest!' There was a pause and then he heard the woman shriek:

'May the gods curse you!' She muttered something in a language he could not understand.

As soon as he heard the bead curtain rattle again, Lupus quickly ran off to follow Avitus.

After Avitus left the soothsayer, he went straight to a tavern. Lupus rounded the corner just in time to see him disappear through the door. It was an inn Lupus was familiar with, and he hesitated a moment before entering.

The Medusa Tavern smelled of sour wine and fish soup. As his eyes grew accustomed to the gloom, Lupus saw several drinkers slouched over trestle tables. Avitus stood at the bar, already draining his first beaker.

Lupus took an empty wine cup from one of the tables, sat cross-legged in the sawdust on the floor, and placed the cup in front of him. Then he hung his head to make himself look more pathetic. He didn't expect to receive any coins, but there were three coppers in his cup by the time Avitus moved unsteadily out of the dim tavern into the blazing heat of the afternoon.

Lupus shadowed Avitus from one inn to the next, all the way to the docks. By the time Avita's father staggered into an inn beside the mouth of the river

Tiber, Lupus had made nearly two sesterces from begging.

The Grain and Grape was a favourite of the soldiers stationed in Ostia: their barracks were nearby. An entire cohort from Rome – six hundred soldiers – patrolled the town in shifts. They worked hard keeping law and order, and guarding against fires. In their spare time, many of them liked to relax at the waterfront taverns with a cup of spiced wine and a game of dice.

A group of off-duty soldiers were there now, gaming with a few civilians at a table overlooking the river harbour. Unlike the other inns Avitus had visited, the Grain and Grape was light and airy. Large open windows offered views of the Mediterranean on one side and the mouth of the Tiber on the other. The late afternoon breeze, which sailors called Venus' Breath, had just started to rise off the sea. It brought a delicious coolness to the inn.

As the gamers called loudly for grilled sausages and honeyed wine, Lupus scanned the room for Avitus: predictably, he was hunched over a drink at the bar.

Hearing the clatter of dice and the laughter of the soldiers, Lupus judged they were in just the right mood to be generous. It would be a shame to miss this opportunity.

Keeping his head down, the beggar-boy approached the soldiers' table, and pitifully held out his empty cup. Most tossed in a few small coins, and one civilian put in half a spiced sausage. Satisfied, Lupus sat on the floor in the sawdust.

Avitus hadn't budged. He was still leaning on the bar pouring wine from a flagon. It was his ninth or tenth drink in under two hours.

Lupus emptied the coins into his cloth pouch and put the empty cup in front of him. He tossed in a coin – one always encouraged more – and munched the sausage carefully.

He found himself thinking about the portrait of Avita, the little girl who had died of a dog bite. He thought of the way the artist had added a tiny white dot to each of her eyes to make them sparkle. He wondered how the paint was made, and how painters were trained. And who were they? Greeks, like the potters? Alexandrians, like the glassmakers? Ephesians, like the silversmiths?

He was studying a fresco of Bacchus and Ceres on the opposite wall when a scuffle broke out at the end of the table nearest to him. A soldier and his young civilian gaming partner were arguing.

The burly soldier grasped a handful of his companion's tunic, pulled him across the table and growled threats into his ear. The others laughed and ignored them, but Lupus saw what they did not: the soldier's dagger glinting beneath the table.

Drops of red liquid spattered onto the sawdust. Lupus stiffened. Then he relaxed as he realised it was only wine; the big soldier had knocked over the civilian's wine cup.

The young man pleaded with the soldier in an urgent whisper. Lupus pricked up his ears, and leaned a little closer.

'. . . at the house of the sea captain Flavius Geminus,' he heard the young man hiss. 'I swear it! A vast treasure! I promise I'll have the money I owe you by tomorrow!'

A vast treasure!

Lupus had never met Flavia's father, but he knew his name was Marcus Flavius Geminus, and that he was a sea captain. There couldn't possibly be two captains by that name in Ostia.

Out of the corner of his eye, Lupus saw the young man relax back onto his bench as the soldier released him. He was well-dressed and, judging from his voice, well-educated, too: probably a young patrician who'd gambled away his allowance. For the next ten years.

The soldier resembled the statue of Hercules near the forum, only bigger and uglier.

'Tomorrow then,' growled the soldier, and Lupus saw the knife go back into its sheath.

Suddenly Lupus remembered what he was supposed to be doing in the tavern. He glanced at the bar, just to make sure the man he was following was still there.

But Avitus had gone.

SCROLL XV

As Jonathan ran up the narrow alley, with Flavia and Nubia close behind him, his mind was racing. Just beyond this warehouse, where the piers ended and the beach began, was the synagogue. Although his family had not been welcome there for several months, he knew it as well as he knew his own house. If only they could get there before the slave-dealers' men caught them.

'Can you see them yet?' he gasped back to Flavia. He was finding it hard to breathe.

'No . . .' he heard her answer, then, 'yes! They're still chasing us!'

Jonathan nearly slipped on something slimy and wet, but he felt Flavia's arm steady him.

'Thanks!' he said, and heard the wheezing in his own voice.

A moment later the three friends shot out of the alley and were nearly trampled by a two-horse carruca. They had come out onto the main coastal road.

'Watch where you're going!' cried the angry driver of the wagon, trying to calm his horses.

'Sorry!' gasped Jonathan over his shoulder.

They ran down the road, overtaking a creaking mule-drawn cart and almost trampling three slaves napping in the shade behind a warehouse.

Jonathan knew exactly where he was going. When he had attended school at the synagogue, he and his friend David had discovered a way out via the courtyard. They would climb onto a branch of the fig tree, walk along the wall, and jump down onto a pile of stone blocks left behind by builders. If only the blocks were still there, he could lead Flavia and Nubia to safety. Once inside the synagogue, they should be safe. Even if the men followed them, Jonathan knew a dozen hiding places.

'Please God, may the blocks be there,' Jonathan prayed silently.

As they rounded the corner of the warehouse, Jonathan breathed a sigh of relief. Although half hidden by weeds, the blocks were visible, still piled against the side wall of the synagogue.

Jonathan sprinted across a short stretch of sandy waste ground and was up the blocks and onto the wall in moments. Straddling the top of the wall and gasping for air, he helped Nubia and Flavia up.

'It's a long drop,' said Flavia dubiously, looking down into the courtyard.

'Along wall . . . to fig tree,' wheezed Jonathan, fighting for breath. 'Then climb down.'

Nubia, holding her arms out like an elegant

tightrope walker, began to move quickly along the top of the wall towards the tree. Flavia followed, scooting rapidly instead of walking. By the time Nubia had reached the tree and had gracefully lowered herself down, Flavia was only halfway there.

'Hurry, Flavia!' gasped Jonathan as he rose to stand on top of the wall.

'I am!' she muttered between gritted teeth.

Flavia stretched forward, grabbed a branch and swung down. For a moment she hung from the fig tree, then dropped down into the courtyard.

'Ow!' she cried. 'My sore ankle.'

Jonathan looked down. The girls' faces seemed very small as they watched him balance on the wall. He felt dizzy and out of breath, but he had done this many times before. Only a few steps and then he would be safe.

He took one faltering step, then another. The trick was not to look directly down, but to fix your eyes on a point some distance ahead.

Another step. He was almost there.

Suddenly he heard a cry to his left. Jonathan's head jerked round: Venalicius's three henchmen had just rounded the corner of the warehouse and had caught sight of him. They were running towards him.

He shouldn't have looked. It broke his concentration and he felt himself losing his balance. Flapping his arms wildly, Jonathan uttered an involuntary cry and tumbled off the wall.

Flavia screamed as Jonathan fell, but by some miracle one of his flailing hands caught a branch and he managed to hold on. For a moment he swung wildly among the leaves, startling a sleeping blackbird which flew up out of the tree with a staccato warning cry. Jonathan reached up with his other hand and grasped the branch. He hung for a moment, wheezing and gasping, trying to think what to do next.

Another shrill scream pierced the air. This time it was Nubia.

An ugly face had appeared over the wall. It was one of Venalicius's men!

The three of them gazed in horrified fascination at his ugly face: he had a broken nose and eyes that pointed in different directions. One eye seemed to be looking at Jonathan, as he dangled from the tree. The other gazed fiercely down at the two girls.

Then the ugly eyes opened wide and he looked past the girls at something behind them.

Flavia and Nubia turned and screamed again.

Looming above them was a huge figure in a black robe and turban.

For a split second, Flavia thought it was Mordecai. Then she realised this man had a longer beard. Also he was taller, heavier and much fiercer-looking.

Venalicius's henchman must have thought so, too: his unpleasant face disappeared back down behind the synagogue wall.

The man in black gave the girls a cold look and then turned his gaze on Jonathan, still hanging limply from the fig tree.

'Shalom, Jonathan,' he said in a dry voice, and then moved underneath the boy and added something in Hebrew.

'Shalom, Rabbi,' wheezed Jonathan. He let go of the branch and fell into the man's strong arms. The rabbi lowered him gently to the ground. Jonathan stood gasping and trying to catch his breath.

The rabbi looked sternly at the girls and said in Latin,

'What are you doing here?'

'I'm sorry, sir,' said Flavia, 'but we were being chased.'

'Yes,' replied the rabbi, 'so it would appear.'

He glanced at Jonathan.

'This boy is not welcome here,' he said tersely. 'His father teaches dangerous lies and has disturbed many.' He looked at Jonathan, who was breathing marjoram oil, and Flavia saw his face soften a fraction.

'It is hard enough for us as it is,' said the rabbi, 'without being associated with these . . .' he hesitated and then said bitterly: '. . . these Christians.'

*

Flavia gasped and looked at Jonathan. 'You're a Christian?'

Jonathan nodded miserably.

Nubia tugged at Flavia's tunic.

'What Christian?' she asked.

'I'll tell you later,' said Flavia grimly.

Jonathan turned to the man in black.

'I'm sorry, Rabbi,' he pleaded, 'we didn't know where else to hide.'

The rabbi's face relaxed and he said to Jonathan,

'I suppose you can't be blamed for your father's misguided beliefs. Besides, the Master of the Universe, blessed be he, tells us to act justly and to love mercy . . .'

He tugged at his thick beard.

'However, I'm afraid there are others who would not be so understanding if they knew you were here. You must leave now.'

Jonathan nodded. 'Of course. We'll go immediately.'

'Just a minute.' The rabbi put his hand on Jonathan's shoulder. 'Let me check to see if it's safe.' He unbolted the double doors on the eastern side of the courtyard and peered out. Then he turned to them.

'No sign of any pursuers,' he said, and held open the doors.

As each of the three passed through the doorway he touched their heads and murmured a blessing.

'Go in peace,' he said gruffly, and then added, 'and go quickly.'

As the synagogue door closed behind them, Jonathan turned to Flavia. 'Which way shall we go?' he asked her.

'They might be waiting for us back at the docks.' Flavia frowned.

'The quickest way home is over the dunes through the graveyard,' said Jonathan.

'But what if we meet the wild dogs again?' asked Flavia nervously.

'Which would you rather meet again?' said Jonathan, starting across the coastal road, 'A few dogs, or those men?'

'A few dogs, I suppose . . .'

'Why didn't you tell us you and your family were Christians?' Flavia asked Jonathan as they set off across the dunes. 'I thought you were Jews.'

The sun threw their shadows ahead of them and a light breeze ruffled their tunics. After a moment Jonathan spoke.

'It's hard to explain. We *are* Jewish, but Christus is the Latin name for our Messiah, so they call us Christians.'

Flavia said in a low voice:

'I've heard that Christians eat their God and my father says they burned Rome the year he put on the toga virilis, the year he was sixteen.'

'That's not true,' said Jonathan angrily. 'Everyone knows Nero only blamed the Christians for burning Rome so that people wouldn't be angry with *him*. Christians are peaceful. We are taught to love our enemies and pray for them.'

'You love your *enemies*?'

'We try to,' Jonathan sighed.

'But isn't it dangerous being a Christian?'

'Yes, it is. We can't worship openly because so many people hate us.' He trudged up a sand dune, wheezing a little, then added bitterly, 'They don't even take the trouble to find out what we believe.'

Flavia was about to ask Jonathan what Christians *did* believe when he stopped short.

'Uh-oh,' he said quietly. They were almost out of the dunes, and he had stopped to look up towards the graveyard. 'Here they come.'

Trotting out of the shimmering heat to meet them, almost like old friends, was a pack of six or seven panting dogs. The friends froze and looked around, but out there on the dunes there was nowhere to run and nowhere to hide.

Lupus rushed out of the tavern and almost collided with Avitus, who was bending over the road. The boy jumped back just in time to avoid being spattered with vomit. Avitus didn't notice the beggar-boy who had been in his daughter's room earlier that day. He wouldn't have noticed a sea nymph riding by on a centaur. He was being violently ill.

Lupus backed off and hid behind a statue of the Emperor Claudius.

Avitus was sick until finally he was retching up nothing. At last he stood, looking pale and haggard, his heavy eyebrows a dark line across his brow. He wiped his sweaty forehead with his arm and turned north towards the new imperial harbour.

It was a beautiful blue afternoon, and as the day cooled, the port was coming to life. Venus' Breath had whipped up the sea beyond the river mouth and it was a deep sapphire colour. The sails of ships moving to and fro on the water made triangles of white and yellow against the blue.

The air was so clear that almost every brick of

the distant lighthouse was visible against the afternoon sky. It was as if Lupus was seeing the
structure for the first time. The tower looked like
three huge red dice piled one on the other, each
smaller than the one below, with a great plume of
smoke furling away from the cylindrical platform at
the very top.

Perhaps Avitus was also seeing the lighthouse as if
for the first time, for presently he set off straight
towards the ferry which would take him across the
Tiber to the new harbour. Somehow, Lupus knew
the little girl's father was heading for the lighthouse.
And somehow, he thought he knew why.

'Sit down on the sand,' said Flavia firmly to her
friends as the dogs approached.

'Sit *down*? Are you mad?' Jonathan's voice was a
bit too shrill. 'A pack of wild dogs are heading
straight for us, about to chew us to pieces and you
say sit down?'

'That's what Pliny says to do,' said Flavia. 'Your
father lent me his book about natural history. Pliny
says, "An angry attack can be averted by sitting on
the ground".'

'Dogs not angry,' said Nubia, gripping Flavia's
arm.

'What do you mean, the dogs aren't angry?'
yelled Jonathan. 'They're wild, rabid, mad, hydro-
phobic killers!'

He pulled his sling from his belt. The slave-girl knew immediately what it was and put a restraining hand on his arm.

'No throw rock. Make dogs angry,' she pleaded.

Jonathan hesitated and then looked to Flavia for guidance. The dogs were almost upon them.

'She's been right about everything else so far,' said Flavia. 'Let's trust her!' She paused. 'And let's trust Pliny, too. Sit down.'

Flavia sat cross-legged on the sand, pulling the other two down beside her. Jonathan closed his eyes and began muttering something in his native language. Flavia suspected he was praying.

The dogs were now so close that she could see their eyes and pink tongues. The lead dog had something in its mouth. Flavia was afraid to look. She closed her eyes but then opened them a crack to peep through. The thing in the dog's mouth looked like a child's arm, or maybe a dirty leg-bone.

She closed her eyes again and waited for the inevitable chomp of jaws on flesh. Now the creatures were so close that she could hear their tongues panting and smell their doggy breath. She stifled a scream as several cold noses prodded and sniffed her, but she felt no pain.

Presently she heard a low growl. The new leader, a brown dog with pointed ears and face, stood before them, his tail wagging. He had dropped the mysterious object on the sand.

Flavia peeked with one eye, then opened the other.

'A stick!' she gasped. 'It's only a stick!' And then, as the realisation dawned, 'They want us to *play* with them, to throw the stick!'

'That's all they've ever wanted!' laughed Jonathan, and Nubia began to laugh, too.

'And we thought they wanted to kill us!'

With tears of laughter and relief flowing down her face, Flavia knelt and reached for the stick. The leader watched, alert and panting eagerly. Flavia stood, drew back her arm as far as she could and then threw the stick towards the blue line of the sea beyond the dunes.

Like arrows released from a bow, the dogs were after it, barking and yelping with delight.

'Run!' laughed Jonathan, scrambling to his feet and helping Nubia up.

The three of them ran as fast as they could away from the dogs, towards the tombs.

But before they had reached the harder ground which bordered the necropolis, the dogs were back again, surrounding them.

Again, the leader dropped the stick. This time, however, Flavia reached for it too quickly. The leader lunged forward snarling, and almost seized her hand.

'Oh!' cried Flavia, 'I startled him!'

'Let Nubia do it,' said Nubia softly. She reached

for the stick carefully, and threw it hard towards the sea. Again the dogs went one way and the children the other.

Again, they were soon surrounded by the dogs.

'Now it's not so funny,' gasped Flavia, as she threw the stick again. 'At this rate, it will take us hours to get home.'

'And the sun will be setting soon,' added Jonathan, whose asthma was making him wheeze again. 'Father will murder me when I get back.'

'Cheer up, maybe the dogs will kill you first,' joked Flavia, and was relieved to see Jonathan grin back.

Once again they were surrounded by a solid, panting mass of dogs and presented with a wet stick.

It was Jonathan's turn to throw the stick. He gingerly picked up the sopping piece of driftwood and allowed some of the saliva to drip off it. 'What does Pliny say about mad dog's slobber?' he asked, wrinkling his nose.

The leader growled. The dogs were becoming more and more impatient, more and more demanding. Something had to be done.

'Nubia has idea,' ventured the slave-girl, 'of escape from dogs.' The others turned and looked at her hopefully.

Just as Lupus was about to slip through the gate of the low wall surrounding the lighthouse, one of the guards playing dice looked up.

'Hey, you!' he bellowed, jumping to his feet. 'Get away from here!' The other two glanced over. They looked bored.

Lupus grunted in protest and pointed urgently at the lighthouse. Avitus had passed through the gate unchallenged only a moment before. The soldiers had been so intent on their game that they hadn't noticed him.

'I said get out!' The guard lumbered over and thrust his face into Lupus's. His breath reeked of garlic and his tunic stank of sweat.

Lupus lowered his arm, and then opening his eyes wide as if in surprise, he pointed again. At last the guard turned to look, but Avitus had just disappeared into the lower entrance of the tower.

Lupus let his shoulders slump and turned as if to go. Then he whirled around and darted through the gate while the soldier's guard was down.

Lupus was quick, but the soldier was quicker, and Lupus felt the air knocked out of him as the soldier grabbed his belt from behind. The other two guards rose to their feet and sauntered over.

'Look, you!' said Garlic-breath, holding Lupus aloft by his belt. 'I'm going to count to ten and when I finish I don't want to see your snotty little face anywhere around here. Or else I'll throw you in the harbour. *Do you understand?*' He dropped Lupus onto the hard concrete of the breakwater.

On his hands and knees, Lupus nodded, and

glanced quickly up at the lighthouse. There must be slaves at the top to feed the fire, but he couldn't see anyone. A great plume of black smoke was being fanned towards the town by the stiffening offshore breeze. From this close, the top seemed an immense height above him.

At that moment, Lupus saw Avitus appear on the second level. He seemed very high up.

Lupus scrambled to his feet and tried pointing again, but the soldier had already begun counting in a loud voice: 'six, seven, eight – .'

'Wait, Grumex!' said one of the other soldiers. 'I think I just saw someone up there.'

Garlic-breath whirled round, but Avitus had disappeared again. They all squinted up at the red brick tower, looking for movement. Apart from the smoke billowing far above them and a few gliding seagulls, there was nothing. In the silence, Lupus could hear the waves slapping against the breakwater and he felt a fine spray on the side of his face.

'You're crazy!' said Grumex after a few moments, but he sounded doubtful. 'Better go and check anyway . . .' he added after a moment. Then, noticing Lupus, he snarled,

'Go on! Get out of here!'

Lupus was backing off when suddenly, behind him, a woman carrying a fishing net screamed. At the edge of the highest tier of the lighthouse, a figure stood silhouetted against the sky.

'A man!' the woman shrieked, dropping her net and pointing. 'There's a man on the lighthouse and I think he's going to jump!'

The dogs' leader growled low in his throat. Jonathan dropped the slimy stick and looked at Nubia.

'OK,' he said. 'What's your idea?'

The slave-girl closed her eyes.

She began to hum: softly at first, then louder. Then she took a deep breath and started to sing a strange, tuneless song. It made the fine hairs at the back of Flavia's neck stand up. The dogs began to whimper. Presently one or two of them sat.

Nubia was singing a song her father had taught her: the Dog-Song. She sang the story of how dogs had once been like jackals, wolves and desert foxes, hunting in the cold night. She reminded the dogs of how their ancestors used to howl at the moon from loneliness and hunger and a yearning for something they had never known.

The dogs began to howl with Nubia. Jonathan and Flavia exchanged wide-eyed looks, then turned back to watch her in fascination.

Gradually Nubia's song changed. She began to

croon the story-song, relating how dogs discovered man and fire and warmth and safety. How they no longer had to roam cold and hungry at night, but could curl up beside the fire with a full belly and someone to scratch them behind their ears.

The dogs had stopped howling now, and were settling down. One or two were actually lying on the ground panting, their eyes half closed. The others were sitting. The leader whined and half stood, as if he felt his power fading.

But now Nubia was singing of warmth and love and loyalty and devotion, and finally he too settled down, rested his sharp, brown muzzle on his paws, and listened.

Bathed in the red light of the setting sun, the sea was the colour of purple wine. Lupus knew his friends would have been expecting him for some time now, but he could not leave the great curving breakwater on which the lighthouse stood.

Quite a crowd had gathered by now. The lighthouse was a dark shape against the blood-red sun, and the great plume of smoke from the bonfire at its top was as black as ink.

A hundred feet above them stood two tiny figures, silhouetted against the fading sky. One was poised at the very edge of the platform. The other figure, a soldier, stood on the same level, but further away. Every time he started to move, the man on the edge swayed forward as if to jump, and the crowd gasped.

A centurion was moving through the crowd asking if anyone knew who the man on the lighthouse was. Lupus considered trying to catch his eye, but even if he managed to communicate with him, what would he say? That the man's name was Avitus? That he was consumed with grief for his dead daughter and had been drinking wine all afternoon? What good would that do?

Lupus hung his head as the officer pushed past. But he needn't have bothered: the centurion didn't even glance at him.

The crowd suddenly gasped again and Lupus looked up. High above them, the soldier was finally approaching Avitus with his hand extended.

It was at that moment that the tiny black figure swaying on the edge silently pitched forward and fell through space. There was a cry from the onlookers as the figure struck the edge of the first tier, bounced and tumbled like a rag doll down to the concrete below.

Humming softly, Nubia stepped carefully around the dogs. Flavia and Jonathan followed her. Resisting the urge to run, the three friends made their way through the necropolis, now full of long, purple shadows. Behind them, the dogs sat or lay, almost as if they had been drugged. One, a heavily pregnant bitch, followed them for a while and then turned back with a wistful whine.

Flavia suddenly realised she was so thirsty she could hardly swallow. She tried not to think how wonderful a cup of cool water would taste. She would even drink the water at the green fountain, though it always tasted slightly mouldy.

Up the dusty road the three of them went, past trees whose leaves glowed like emeralds in the light of the setting sun, past the cooling glade where Avita was buried, past the tomb of fighting gladiators, and on through Fountain Gate.

As soon as they had passed beneath its arch, they knew they were safe. Without a word, they ran to the green-tiled fountain in the centre of the cross-roads and plunged their dusty faces into the cold water. Then, each chose a spout and drank deeply. Flavia had never tasted anything as delicious as that water, even with its slight taint.

At last they turned their tired feet for home, dreading the reception they would get.

Rounding the corner, they were surprised to find a group of soldiers standing outside Cordius's house. An official-looking person, a magistrate, was deep in discussion with Libertus himself. Several passers-by had stopped to watch. Among them Flavia noticed the fat merchant in the grubby toga whom she'd seen laughing with Venalicius at the slave market.

Suddenly Libertus glanced up and saw Flavia.

'Those are the children I was telling you about!' she heard him say to the official. The young freedman smiled and beckoned them over.

'Their dog was killed, too,' Libertus was telling the magistrate, 'and beheaded! Just like Ruber!' He turned his dark blue eyes on Flavia. 'Avitus has just killed Ruber!'

'Ruber? Who's Ruber?' asked Flavia. But at that moment Cordius's front door opened and two soldiers emerged. Between them walked the sour doorkeeper who had let the girls in earlier that morning. Tears streamed down his hollow cheeks and in his arms he carried the headless body of a red hound.

'These children know who killed the dogs!' Libertus repeated to the magistrate. 'They know the man who knocked my porter unconscious and killed my watchdog. They know his name and even have a portrait of him on a wax tablet.'

'But – ' said Flavia.

'Your dog was killed as well?' asked the magistrate. 'And you think you know who did it?' He was a short man with thinning hair and pale, intelligent eyes.

'Well . . .' began Flavia, thinking of Avitus sobbing in his wife's arms and writing poetry about dolphins. 'We're not *positive* – '

'I still think he did it,' said Jonathan.

'And so do I!' agreed Libertus. 'I saw him running away from this boy's house yesterday, and it must be the same man who killed my dog. There can't be two dog-killers on the same street!' He turned to Flavia. 'Do you still have the drawing?'

Flavia pulled the wax tablet from her belt and showed the magistrate Lupus's sketch.

'He lives just up the road and his name is Publius Avitus Proculus,' said Jonathan firmly. 'His daughter was killed by a mad dog several weeks ago.'

'Well,' said the magistrate to the captain of the soldiers, 'I think we'd better interview this Avitus. Can you take us to his house, young man?'

'Yes, I can,' said Jonathan importantly, and led the way up the road to the house with the red door. Then he stood back while the magistrate pounded the knocker. Gradually the small crowd grew silent, and fixed their eyes on the door, waiting for some- one – perhaps even the dog-killer himself – to answer.

As they waited, Flavia felt a touch on her arm. Nubia was pointing to the mulberry tree. On its trunk was scrawled a faint chalk arrow: it pointed north, towards the Roman Gate.

'That means Lupus *did* follow Avitus,' whispered Flavia. 'I wonder if he's back yet?'

'You wonder if who's back yet?' said a man's voice behind her.

Flavia jumped, then relaxed to see it was only Mordecai.

'Peace be with you.' He gave his little bow. 'Where is Jonathan?' he asked, 'and what is going on?'

'He's right there, by those soldiers.' Flavia pointed. 'He's helping the magistrate. Cordius's watchdog has just been killed and beheaded.'

At that moment the red door opened and the crowd held their collective breath. In the darkening twilight, Flavia could just make out Julia, Avitus's wife, at the door. They all saw her shake her head.

It was becoming too dark for any further investigation. Slaves were lighting lamps in the houses nearby. The magistrate and the soldiers marched past them back to their barracks.

Mordecai glowered at them as they passed.

'I spent nearly one whole day in a clerk's office only to be told nothing could be done,' he grumbled. 'But when a rich man's watchdog is killed the crime is under investigation within minutes!'

'Father!' cried Jonathan, running up. Mordecai was surprised to find his son's arms around him. 'Father, don't be angry!'

Flavia secretly gave Jonathan's arm a pinch. 'Your father has only just now returned,' she said with a significant look. She didn't want him to tell Mordecai they had broken their promise.

'Why should I be angry?' asked the doctor.

'Er, no reason,' Jonathan said. 'It's just that our house key is still at Flavia's!' Mordecai looked sharply at Jonathan, so Flavia said quickly,

'What did you find out from the magistrate?'

'Well,' said the doctor, as they began to walk back down the street, 'he told me the dogs here in Ostia aren't truly wild. Most of them used to be tame, but their masters either died or abandoned them. They became feral, that is half-wild, and they began to run together in a pack. One clerk I spoke with said they weren't really dangerous, but just a nuisance.

'He also told me that dogs with hydrophobia, or mad dogs, always run alone. Because, you see, even the other dogs are afraid of them.'

The street had emptied and total darkness had descended by the time they reached Flavia's house. The double doors of Cordius's house opposite had been shut and bolted. Two blazing torches had been set on either side. They lit up the porch as if it were day.

'Should we light our torches, too?' said Flavia, almost to herself.

'No need,' said Mordecai, 'Cordius no longer has a watchdog, but you still do.'

An awful thought suddenly struck Flavia and Nubia at the same time and they looked at each other fearfully.

'I *hope* we still have a watchdog!' cried Flavia, and pounded hard on her door.

SCROLL XVIII

Flavia banged the bronze figure of Castor hard against the bronze Pollux again and again, frantically calling Caudex.

'Listen!' said Nubia suddenly, putting her hand on Flavia's arm.

From deep inside the house they heard the wonderful sound of Scuto's bark.

A moment later Caudex slid open the peephole and blinked sleepily at them. Now they could hear Scuto's claws scrabbling on the inside of the door.

'Open up, Caudex!' cried Flavia. 'We're hungry and tired and, oh hurry!'

At last the door swung open and Scuto joyfully greeted everyone, licking and pawing and wagging his tail. Even Mordecai got a sloppy wet kiss. As they all moved into the atrium Alma bustled up, scolding them for being so late.

'What do you mean, staying out after dark?' she cried, hugging Flavia hard. 'I nearly died of worry.' She gave Nubia a squeeze and complained, 'Caudex was beside himself, too. Weren't you, Caudex?'

The slave yawned and nodded.

'I've made enough dinner for you all,' Alma announced. 'Come and eat it before it gets cold.'

Jonathan was hanging back, hoping to avoid Alma's enthusiastic welcome, but she caught sight of him and enveloped him in a squishy embrace.

'And where's Wolfie?' she asked, looking hopefully past Mordecai and out through the open door.

'Isn't Lupus back yet?' cried Flavia.

'No, not a trace of him,' frowned Alma.

They were all sitting around the table, just finishing their soup, when Scuto uttered a loud bark, leapt up from under Nubia's feet and scampered out of the dining room. A few minutes later he trotted back with a tired and hungry Lupus in tow. Flavia quickly drew up another chair and Alma brought the boy a bowl of warm broth, the last of the chicken soup.

The others waited for Lupus to finish before they began their fish and leek pie.

'We have news for you!' Flavia said, as Lupus pushed away his empty soup bowl.

Lupus pointed at himself and then back at her, as if to say, And I have news for you, too!

'Do you remember we told you about the red watchdog we saw at Cordius's house this morning?'

Lupus nodded and took a bite of fish pie.

'Well, someone killed him a few hours ago!' breathed Flavia. 'And they cut off his head!'

'Like Bobas. Dog of Jonathan,' added Nubia.

Lupus choked on his mouthful and had to be pounded on the back by the doctor, who was sitting beside him.

When Lupus had recovered, Mordecai turned to Flavia.

'You went to Cordius's house?'

'Yes, Nubia and I went this morning. We wanted to speak to his freedman Libertus, because he is our only witness. Remember he was standing at the fountain just before we found Bobas's body?'

'Yes,' said Mordecai slowly.

'Well, while he was at the fountain, Libertus saw a man running away from your house. The man was carrying a bag, and it could have had a head inside.'

'Like Perseus,' said Nubia.

Flavia continued,

'Nubia and I went round to Libertus's house this morning, and he said that the man in the drawing was the man he saw that day. The running man was Avitus!'

'Wait.' Mordecai looked confused. 'What drawing?'

'This drawing.' Flavia showed him the wax tablet, now very smudged but still quite recognisable. 'Lupus drew it.'

'You drew this?' Mordecai asked in amazement, taking the tablet. 'It's excellent!'

'That was the man we saw crying in the graveyard. Lupus knew who he was and drew him,' explained Flavia.

'It must have been Avitus who killed the dogs!' exclaimed Jonathan.

Lupus made a strangled noise and when they looked at him he was violently shaking his head.

'Let's see what Lupus has to report,' said Flavia. 'You followed Avitus today, didn't you? We saw your chalk arrow on the tree.'

Lupus nodded. All eyes were on him.

'How soon after we left you did Avitus come out of his house?'

Lupus held his thumb and forefinger close together.

'A short time?'

Lupus nodded.

'And what did he do?' asked Mordecai, with great interest.

Lupus imitated someone drinking and then becoming drunk. He held up five fingers.

'He had five beakers of wine?' asked Flavia.

Lupus shook his head and held up ten fingers.

'Ten beakers of wine!' shouted Jonathan.

Lupus nodded emphatically.

'He had ten beakers of wine?' said Flavia, amazed. 'And what's the five?'

Lupus made his fingers walk around the table: first they walked onto Nubia's empty plate, then onto Jonathan's plate, then Flavia's.

'Five taverns!' shouted Jonathan.

Lupus nodded.

'But ten beakers!' exclaimed Mordecai. 'A man wouldn't be able to walk after drinking that amount.'

Lupus imitated someone throwing up. They all wrinkled their noses and nodded.

'He could still have killed Ruber the watchdog,' insisted Jonathan, 'maybe in a drunken haze.'

Lupus shook his head and drew the side of his hand across his throat. They all stared at him in silence. Then Flavia whispered:

'He's dead?'

Lupus nodded.

'Avitus?' asked Jonathan.

Lupus nodded again.

'How?'

Lupus walked his fingers up the wine jug and then made them jump off and splat onto the table.

'Where?' asked Mordecai. His voice was grave.

Lupus looked around and then caught sight of the wax tablet. He rubbed out his drawing of Avitus and with the tip of his knife he scratched something into the wax.

Mordecai took it, nodded and showed it to the others.

'The lighthouse!' breathed Flavia. She looked at up Lupus, 'And you saw him jump?'

Lupus nodded gravely.

'Then that means Avitus couldn't have killed Ruber,' said Flavia slowly. 'He hasn't been near our street all afternoon. But if he didn't do it, who did?'

Everyone was too tired to think clearly. Flavia and Jonathan were yawning over their dessert of apples stewed in honey and pepper. Nubia had actually fallen asleep in her chair.

'Come, Jonathan,' said Mordecai. 'We must go home to bed now. Lupus, will you be our guest again tonight?'

In reply, Lupus looked at Flavia, raised his eyebrows and pointed down.

'You'd like to spend the night here?' asked Flavia. 'Of course! Alma, may Lupus spend the night here?'

Alma was clearing away the dinner plates.

'Of course, dear. He can sleep in Aristo's bedroom.'

'Very well,' said Mordecai. 'We will say goodnight. Peace be with you.'

'I'll just fetch your house key,' said Alma and disappeared into the study.

After Jonathan and his father had left, Caudex bolted the door after them. A yawning Nubia had already disappeared into the garden with Scuto, so Flavia showed Lupus to the spare room.

'Here's a clay lamp for you,' she said, 'I always keep one lit in my room. There's a copper beaker of cold water on that shelf and a chamber-pot under the bed, in case you can't be bothered to go downstairs to the latrine in the middle of the night.'

Although Flavia was utterly exhausted, she couldn't sleep. The house was quiet and dark. Everyone had gone to bed. Lupus had begun snoring even before she was out of the bedroom. Nubia was snuggled up with Scuto under the fig tree in the garden. Alma and Caudex were sleeping in their rooms off the atrium. Outside, in the graveyard, the tree-frogs had taken over from the cicadas and were croaking slowly and rhythmically, as if urging her to sleep.

The rising moon shone through the lattice screen of her window and made silver diamonds on her bedroom wall. There was even a sea breeze drifting in from the south to soothe her. It smelled of pine and salt water, and made her think of the ocean.

She thought of her father, somewhere far out on the inky waves, perhaps pacing the deck and gazing at the same moon that shone through her window. She offered up a prayer to Neptune, god of the sea.

Then she turned her thoughts to the events of the past days. Had it only been two?

Poor Avitus was dead now, unable to live with his grief, and it was suddenly clear to her that he had never killed the dogs. He hadn't even been able to hit Scuto with a pine cone. How could he have coolly killed and beheaded Bobas?

But that brought her back to the puzzle that was

keeping her awake. If Avitus hadn't killed Bobas and Ruber, who had? And who had taken the mastiff's head away from the graveyard?

Outside in the necropolis she heard an owl hooting. People said owls were bad luck, but her father always called her his 'little owl' and so she liked them. Besides, the owl was the bird of Minerva, the goddess of wisdom.

Wisdom made her think of Aristo, the young Greek who had been her tutor for the past two years. She tried to think in the way he had taught her: using both logic and imagination.

'If Avitus didn't kill the dogs, then who did?' she thought. 'We first thought Avitus killed them because he hated all dogs. But if someone else killed the dogs, they probably had another reason. Why would someone want to kill dogs?'

At that moment Scuto began barking downstairs, and as his barks set off all the other dogs in the neighbourhood, Flavia suddenly had the answer. She sat up in her bed.

'Of course!' she breathed. 'That's why!'

But just then she heard Nubia scream.

SCROLL XIX

'Thief!' said Nubia, as Flavia hurried down the stairs, carefully holding her lamp. 'Thief!' she repeated, and pointed to the storeroom. Flavia saw what had alarmed her: there was a sliver of light all around the edge of the storeroom door.

Scuto was wagging his tail and sniffing at the door. He barked again cheerfully.

Caudex ambled into the garden, carrying a torch and looking no more sleepy than he did the rest of the time.

'Caudex!' cried Flavia. 'There's a thief in the storeroom!'

'Nothing in there worth taking,' mumbled the slave. 'Just grain and wine and some bits of old furniture . . .'

'Person go in there!' said Nubia.

'And I can see a light!' insisted Flavia.

Caudex squinted at the door, and scratched his head.

'All right,' he said with a shrug, and moved towards the door. The flames of his torch threw flickering bars of shadow from the columns onto the wall. Flavia and Nubia clung to each other as Caudex cautiously opened the door, and Scuto wagged his tail.

'What's all this noise?' Alma padded in, carrying a clay lamp. She was barefoot and had tied her hair up with a scarf. The lamp, lighting her face eerily from below, made her look like a stranger.

'There's a thief in the storeroom!' said Flavia, 'and I'm sure it's the person who killed the dogs.'

Suddenly, from the storeroom came two yells, one high and one low. Scuto, standing just outside the doorway, began to bark again.

'Got him!' they heard Caudex grunt, and then in a slightly muffled voice. 'Got your thief.'

He emerged from the storeroom. In one hand he held the flaming torch, and in the other he carried a squirming boy.

'Lupus!' exclaimed Flavia and Nubia together.

Lupus was struggling in Caudex's grip and incoherent sounds were coming out of his mouth. The words were garbled, but the sense of them was clear: Put me down, you big oaf!

'Caudex! Put him down!' cried Flavia. 'Lupus isn't a thief!'

Lupus's eyes blazed green in the torchlight, but Caudex did not put him down. Instead, he set the torch into one of the brackets on the wall. Then he took Lupus in both hands, held him upside down by the ankles, and gave him a good shake. Flavia and Nubia squealed and covered their eyes: Lupus's tunic had flopped down and he was wearing nothing underneath.

Then they heard the jingle of coins on marble and they opened their eyes in astonishment.

When Caudex had finished shaking Lupus down, he set the boy on his feet. Lupus stood hanging his head in shame: there on the walkway bordering the garden lay a dozen gold coins, glowing and winking in the flickering torchlight.

They all stared at Lupus in dismay. The coins on the marble pathway and his miserable expression confirmed his guilt.

'Lupus!' whispered Flavia after a moment. 'Where did you find that gold? Was it in the storeroom?'

Lupus nodded.

'Then you *were* stealing from us. We trusted you and opened our home to you and . . . THAT'S IT!'

They all stared at her, even Lupus raised his head.

'I think I've solved the crime!' cried Flavia.

She turned to Lupus.

'Lupus, you've *got* to help us. Where did you find that gold and how did you know it was here? We never keep that much gold in the house.'

Lupus glared at her. He was deeply ashamed and embarrassed.

'Please, Lupus! Everything makes sense now. We'll forget that you tried to steal the money, if only you'll help us!'

Lupus gestured sullenly for them to follow him. Caudex took the torch from the wall. The girls and Alma took their lamps, and they all followed Lupus back into the storeroom.

The boy led them to three large amphoras near the darkest corner. The jars were half-buried to keep them standing upright and looked just like all the others, except that they were set a little apart. One of them was closed but not sealed. Flavia went to this amphora and removed the lid.

Everyone gasped. This big jar did not contain grain or wine or olive oil like the rest. It was filled nearly to the brim with gold coins.

'Why, it's enough to buy our house a dozen times over,' breathed Flavia, dipping her hand in and letting the heavy coins sift through her fingers. 'And look! This seal isn't ours.' She picked up a blue wax seal about the size of a coin which had fallen to the storeroom floor. She held it up to her lamp and examined it. 'It's not the twins. It's a dolphin!'

'That'll be the seal of Cordius, your father's patron,' said Alma. 'Perhaps he didn't have enough room for all his treasure and asked Captain Geminus to store some of it.'

'Alma, I think you're right!' said Flavia. 'This

treasure certainly isn't ours, and the seal is probably Cordius's. But if none of *us* knew it was here, how on earth did Lupus know?'

She turned to the boy, who was still hanging his head.

'Lupus,' she said softly, 'did someone tell you about the treasure?'

Lupus hesitated and then waggled his head, neither nodding or shaking it, but something in between.

'Someone sort of told you about it?' she offered.

He nodded.

'Who?'

Lupus hesitated, then imitated someone drinking.

'Avitus?'

Lupus shook his head and sighed.

'I know! Someone you saw at one of the taverns!'

Lupus nodded.

'Who? Who was it?'

Lupus shrugged.

'Lupus, I think I know who it was but I want to be sure . . .'

Abruptly, Nubia slipped out of the storeroom and reappeared a few moments later with a wax tablet.

'Nubia, you're brilliant!' cried Flavia. 'Lupus, can you draw what he looked like?'

Lupus shrugged again.

'Just do the best you can,' she pleaded. 'Please . . .'

Lupus slowly took the tablet and stylus from Nubia. He squatted on the sandy floor of the storeroom and started to draw. Everyone moved their torches closer, so that he could see as clearly as possible. Lupus stopped, scratched his head thoughtfully, rubbed out the lower half and started again.

Finally he finished and held the tablet out to Flavia. She took it with a trembling hand and looked at the face he had drawn.

'I knew it!' she breathed. 'It had to be him. I should have guessed before.'

She had solved the mystery, but nothing could be done about it until morning. Flavia crawled back into bed and was sure she would lie awake all night going over the clues in her mind.

But she was wrong. She fell asleep the moment her head touched the pillow, and soon she began to dream.

She dreamt about Avita Procula.

In the dream, the little girl was being chased by wild dogs. Suddenly a huge magpie flew down and carried Avita up into the air. Avita was laughing and waving at Flavia who stood on the ground. As Flavia watched the girl disappear into the heavens, she realised the dogs were now coming towards her. She turned and ran, but although her heart was pounding she ran slowly, as if she were moving through sticky honey.

In her dream she heard the dogs' barking grow closer and imagined she felt their hot breath on her legs. She had dreamt this dream before and she knew she always woke just as the animals leapt for her with open jaws. But this time something was different. Without turning around, she realised that there was now only one dog pursuing her: one dog with three horrible heads. Cerberus, the hound from hell. In her dream she heard someone screaming again and again, and the screaming didn't stop.

Flavia woke up sweating. Her heart was pounding and her whole body trembling. She was groggy and confused and wondered how she could be awake when she still heard screaming.

It was an awful scream, a woman's hysterical expression of pure horror. Strangely, it sounded like Alma.

Flavia swung her feet out of bed, but she was clumsy and half-asleep, and she banged her toe on the bedside table. Automatically, she took up her clay lamp before she stumbled out onto the balcony.

The moon was almost directly overhead. It poured a wash of eerie light onto the garden below, making the shadows inky black. By the stars in the sky and the damp in the air, Flavia knew it was the middle of the night.

She stood hesitating, and while she stood, she heard a man's cry, short and involuntary. Caudex?

Although she was trembling, she made her way carefully downstairs and crossed the garden by the moonlit path. The pebbles hurt her bare feet but she didn't want the dangerous black shadows behind the columns to touch her.

'Nubia?' she whispered. 'Alma?'

Up ahead a flickering light moved and the scent of a pitch pine torch reached her nose. Another moan echoed from the atrium. The corridor looked like a gaping throat ready to swallow her with shadows, so she ran down it as fast as she could. A wave of relief swept over her as she saw four familiar figures and one dog silhouetted by the orange light of a torch.

They were standing at the open front door and when they heard her feet pattering on the marble floor of the atrium they all turned to look at her.

In each of their faces was reflected a different kind of horror. Even Scuto was whimpering. They were so stunned that none of them made a move to stop Flavia from looking at the thing in the street. She passed between Nubia, who was trembling, and Lupus, who crouched like an animal about to flee. Flavia stopped in the doorway.

There in the moon-washed street stood a trident, the kind fishermen use to catch fish. Its base was wedged tight between paving stones and its three prongs pointed up towards the cold stars. On each of the three points was planted a severed dog's head.

One was white, one black, and one red. Each pair of milky, blind eyes was staring directly at Flavia.

She heard a scream and realised it was coming from her own throat. A wave of black nausea washed over her as the unseeing eyes of the hounds impaled on the trident stared into hers. The dogs' heads filled her vision and became the three heads of the undead creature who guarded the underworld. The blood pounded in her ears like rhythmic thunder as the heads of Cerberus receded until they were three points at the end of a long tunnel. Finally, even the three pin-sized heads were snuffed out and she was sucked down after them into the darkness.

SCROLL XX

'Flavia? Flavia, are you all right?'

A familiar accented voice sounded in Flavia's ear. She kept her eyes closed for a minute, considering the red-brown light beyond her eyelids. Was it morning? It still felt like night. Then she smelled oil-lamps and cinnamon and mint tea, and Flavia knew she was safe in Jonathan's house.

She opened her eyes to see Mordecai standing over her with a gentle smile. His hair hung loose and long about his shoulders.

'What happened?' Flavia asked him.

'You fainted,' the doctor explained.

'Then it wasn't a dream?'

'I'm afraid not. The thing you saw was real.' Mordecai held out a cup of steaming mint tea and urged, 'Drink this.'

Flavia sipped the hot, sweet drink and looked around. She was in Mordecai's study on the striped divan, propped up by cushions. The room was blazing with light. She guessed he had lit every candle and lamp in the house.

Nubia was sitting on the floor with Scuto,

hugging an orange blanket around them both. Jonathan stood nearby, looking pale and concerned. Alma perched on the edge of the divan. She, too, was wrapped in a thick blanket and sipping mint tea.

'That's right, drink the tea,' said Mordecai gently to Flavia. It occurred to her that mint tea was Mordecai's cure-all. It would be easy to be a doctor: you just had to know how to brew mint tea. She smiled at the thought.

'That's better.' Mordecai helped Flavia sit up a bit more.

'Where's Lupus?' she asked suddenly.

Jonathan and his father exchanged quick looks. Mordecai answered softly:

'Alma told us what happened: how you found him stealing the gold . . .'

'He's gone!' Jonathan blurted out. 'He just ran out into the night after we came to see what had happened.'

'Did you see Cerberus? I mean the *thing*?' Flavia couldn't bring herself to say the words.

'Yes,' said Jonathan, swallowing and looking sick. 'Alma told us how she heard a moan outside her window, and when she looked out . . . Some fiend had stuck Bobas's head, and Ruber's and the missing head from the graveyard, on a trident.' He shivered in the flickering candlelight.

'Caudex is taking the . . . three heads through the

house to put outside in the graveyard,' said Mordecai. 'He'll bury them tomorrow.'

'I thought I had gone to the land of the dead. Or that it was some horrible nightmare,' Flavia whispered.

'It wasn't a nightmare!' said Alma suddenly, putting her cup down decisively and rising to her feet. 'It was real and it was an omen of death!' There was a note of hysteria in her voice. 'Tomorrow we are leaving this town until your father returns!'

'No!' cried Flavia, sitting forward. 'That's exactly what the killer wants. He wants to frighten us away so that he can get at the gold.' She chewed her lower lip thoughtfully. 'But we must *pretend* to go away. Yes! That's it! We'll set a trap for the thief.' She took a gulp of the sweet tea.

'Tomorrow we'll all pack and make a big show of leaving. But we'll leave the back door unbolted. We'll go out of the city gate, then double back through the graveyard and keep watch. Then, when he comes, we pounce!'

Caudex came in, looking slightly queasy and wiping his hands on his tunic.

'Who will we pounce on?' he asked thickly.

'The thief, of course,' said Flavia. 'But we need some way of proving his guilt. Something which will prove beyond a doubt he was after the money . . .' Suddenly she remembered the magpie's inky footprint on her father's parchment.

'Doctor Mordecai,' she said excitedly, 'do you have a medicine or potion which would stain someone's hands?'

Mordecai thought for a moment and then his face lit up.

'Yes,' he said. 'I have just the thing to catch your thief . . .'

'But who *is* the thief?' asked Jonathan, bursting with curiosity.

'Yes, who?' they all echoed.

'Do you mean you haven't guessed yet?' asked Flavia, and the sparkle returned to her eyes.

The next day around noon, a two-horse carruca clattered up Green Fountain Street and stopped in front of the house of Marcus Flavius Geminus. The blue door of the house swung open, and the door of the neighbouring house, too, and for the next half hour people moved noisily in and out of the two houses, packing the carriage with chests and travel bags.

Up and down the street shutters squeaked open as curious neighbours satisfied themselves that nothing was amiss. A family was just going on a trip. Those who peeped out saw an oriental-looking man in a black turban directing a large slave in the loading of a cart. They heard the voices of children and the snorting and stamping of horses. Presently the neighbours closed their shutters again and returned to their midday siestas.

When the luggage was stowed in the carruca, a rather plump female climbed up beside the driver and sat sobbing noisily into a handkerchief. Three children and a sheep-like dog scrambled up onto the carriage behind the chests. Presently the carruca moved off slowly towards the marina. The big slave and the man with the turban followed on foot.

The clop of the horses' hooves and the grating of the iron-rimmed wheels grew fainter and soon the afternoon throbbed again with heat and the cries of cicadas. Once more Green Fountain Street was quiet and peaceful.

The carruca rattled away from Flavia's house towards the marina. As it passed the Laurentum Gate, Flavia and Jonathan slipped off the back of the carriage and landed lightly on the street.

'Look after Scuto, Nubia,' whispered Flavia.

'Look after Nubia, Scuto,' grinned Jonathan.

The cart clattered and creaked on its way. Caudex continued to walk behind it, but Mordecai joined Flavia and Jonathan as they hurried towards the brick arch of the gate.

'Where is he?' muttered Flavia, looking around nervously.

'Here I am.' A figure stepped out from behind

one of the columns which flanked the arch. It was the magistrate they had seen the previous afternoon. His pale eyes looked them over.

'Marcus Artorius Bato,' he said, introducing himself. 'I received your message. Your charge is a serious one.'

'Yes, we know,' replied Mordecai, 'and we pray that we are not wasting your time.'

'So do I,' said the young man drily. 'Lead on.'

'This way!' said Flavia, and led them out of the gate and back along the outside of the city wall. They moved quickly, pushing through the dry grasses and thistles, startling dozens of tiny brown grasshoppers. They soon crossed the dusty road which led back into the city through Fountain Gate and stood at Flavia's back door.

Bato shook his head disapprovingly.

'There's a regulation against building into the city walls, you know. This door should be blocked up.'

'We're not the only ones.' Flavia gestured towards Jonathan's door.

'Thanks, Flavia.' Jonathan glared at her.

'We'll block up our doors if necessary,' said Mordecai politely, 'but just now we have a thief to catch!'

Bato gave a curt nod.

Flavia had left the back door wedged open with a twist of old papyrus. Now she put her eye to a gap

166

about the width of her little finger. Between the columns surrounding her garden she could just see the storeroom door.

Jonathan crouched down below her to look, too. He wobbled a little and put out his hand to steady himself.

'Careful!' hissed Flavia. 'If you push the door shut we'll be locked out and we'll never catch him!'

'Sorry!' Jonathan grinned sheepishly.

'It may be a long wait,' said Flavia, glancing up at the young magistrate.

'As if I have nothing better to do,' Bato remarked sarcastically, mopping his forehead with a cloth. It was like an oven in the midday sun.

'I suggest that Marcus Artorius Bato and I wait in the shade of that pine,' whispered Mordecai. 'You two can take turns keeping watch . . .'

'No, wait!' breathed Flavia, putting up her hand. 'He's there!' She gazed up at them in wonder: her trap had worked!

'What's he doing?' mouthed Jonathan.

Flavia put her eye to the crack again.

'He's in the study . . . looking behind scrolls, under the desk . . . He's being very careful: trying not to disturb anything . . .' She was silent for several moments, moving her head slightly to get the best view.

'What?' cried Jonathan. 'What's he doing now?'

Flavia stood and faced them. Her heart was

thumping and her knees trembling. 'He's just gone into the storeroom,' she breathed. 'This is it!'

Quietly, inch by inch, Flavia began to pull open the back door. Suddenly one of the hinges gave a squeak. Flavia froze. Then she continued opening the door as carefully as she could. Tiny drops of sweat beaded her upper lip and a trickle of it ran down the back of her neck.

At last the door was open enough for each of them to squeeze through. Flavia went last, carefully easing the door shut behind her.

The others waited in the shade of the peristyle, each one standing behind a pillar. It was blessedly cool there and Flavia breathed a sigh of relief. For a moment she pressed her cheek to one of the cool, plaster-covered columns. Then, heart pounding, she began to tiptoe towards the atrium.

'Quick!' she mouthed to the others. 'Through the study to the atrium. We don't want him to get away! Jonathan, you stay here and guard the back door.'

Jonathan nodded and pressed himself behind the column closest to the back door.

Quickly and quietly, the two men followed Flavia past the dining room and into the study. As they moved past the desk, Bato accidentally jogged the pink marble column which held the marble bust of the Emperor. They all froze as the bust slowly wobbled one way and the column the other. Then

Bato reached out and caught the heavy sculpture just as it was about to crash to the marble floor. He set it carefully back on its pedestal and let out a sigh of relief. The stone Vespasian seemed to scowl as the magistrate mopped his forehead again.

They tiptoed forward through the folding doors and into the atrium. At that moment, they heard the storeroom door open and then close. The three of them pressed themselves against the atrium wall. Footsteps moved along the corridor towards them and then, just as they expected the culprit to round the corner, the footsteps stopped.

'By Hercules!' said a man's voice, in a tone of mild surprise.

Bato stepped forward, followed by Mordecai and Flavia.

In the shadow of the corridor stood a man in a yellow tunic, with a heavy leather bag slung round one shoulder. The thief was staring at his hands, which were stained a vivid reddish purple colour. As the three appeared, he raised his head and looked at them with dark blue eyes. It was Libertus.

'Titus Cordius Libertus,' said the magistrate in a loud official voice, 'I arrest you in the name of the Emperor Vespasian, for attempted theft and for destruction of private property.'

Libertus smiled ruefully and gazed at his hands.

'It seems you've caught me red-handed!' he

confessed. He slipped off the bag and eased it to the floor. It settled heavily, the clink of many gold coins muffled by the leather. Flavia and Mordecai glanced at each other.

'Hold out your hands,' commanded Bato.

'What is this?' Libertus asked calmly, referring to the stain on his hands.

'Just a vegetable dye,' replied Mordecai as Bato put stiff leather manacles round the freedman's wrists. 'It will wear off in a few days.'

Jonathan came up behind Libertus. The freedman glanced round at him and gave a puzzled half-smile.

Bato pulled the heavy leather bag from the shadow of the peristyle into the sunny garden and squatted beside it. He opened the leather flap and cautiously poked at the gold with his finger. In the brilliant light they could see that some of the coins were thinly coated with red dye.

'Why did you do it?' Flavia blurted out. The sight of Libertus standing meekly, so handsome and vulnerable, made tears sting her eyes.

'I needed money badly,' he replied quietly. 'And my life depended on getting it quickly.'

'Gambling debts?' Flavia asked, suddenly remembering the dice.

He nodded.

'Why didn't you throw yourself on the mercy of your patron Cordius?' asked Mordecai.

'That stingy old miser wouldn't have given me

anything,' snarled Libertus, and for a moment the bitterness made his face looked ugly. 'That's why he moved all his money over here. So no one could touch it.'

A tear rolled down Flavia's cheek. She swiped at it angrily. Libertus saw her concern and his face relaxed.

'I didn't want to *hurt* anyone,' he said earnestly. 'I just needed some cash.'

Bato looked up sharply. 'The gold in this bag is worth nearly a million sesterces,' he commented dryly.

'And you *did* hurt somebody!' said Jonathan angrily. 'You killed two dogs and nearly frightened us to death.'

'It seemed the best way at the time.' Libertus shrugged. 'I needed to make sure this house was empty long enough for me to search it and to silence that noisy dog next door.'

'Why didn't you just give him a drugged dog biscuit, like the woman in the fresco?' asked Flavia.

'That's a very good question,' remarked Bato, closing the bag and rising to his feet. 'Why did you kill the poor creature? And in such a barbaric manner?'

'I needed him silenced for more than just a few hours,' Libertus replied evenly. 'I removed the head to add an element of fear. Later, when I was investigating the back of this house, I found another dog's head and that gave me my brilliant idea.' For a moment he looked pleased with himself, then he frowned.

'And I almost got away with it.' Libertus glanced resentfully at Mordecai. 'If you hadn't found me out I'd be on my way to Hispania right now, debts paid and with enough money left over to buy a nice little farm . . .'

'You think I found you out?' said Mordecai in surprise, and then laughed. 'No, my dear fellow.' He gestured.

'The person who guessed your plan and set the trap was this young lady here: Flavia Gemina!'

SCROLL XXI

It was late morning. A hot June had become an even hotter July.

The week before, the Emperor Vespasian had passed away with the words 'Oh dear, I think I'm becoming a god.' His son Titus had succeeded him quietly and without bloodshed, much to the relief of all. Flavia's father had already commissioned a sculpture of the young Emperor to join the bust of Vespasian in the study.

Flavia and Nubia were sitting in the garden preparing garlands for the evening celebration. The girls bent their heads, one fair and one dark, over their work. A cool breeze touched Flavia's hair and she brushed a strand from her eyes.

'Look, Nubia,' she said softly, 'you can weave the jasmine into the ivy, and then you put the grape hyacinth in like this. There!' She put her finished garland beside her on the marble bench and counted on her fingers. 'Let's see, how many will we need? One each for me, you, and Jonathan. And Miriam's back now, so that's four. One for my father and one for Doctor Mordecai: that's six. And one for

Cordius. Oh, and Aristo! That's eight. A good number, though nine is the perfect number for a banquet . . .'

'Lupus?' asked Nubia quietly.

'Why do you keep bringing him up?' Flavia scowled. 'He ran away the night he stole – all right, *tried* to steal the gold, and he hasn't come back since. I'm not going to go chasing after a thief. Oh, Pollux! Now look what I've done!' She put down the ruined garland and stared at it absently.

Scuto, lying at their feet, pricked up his ears, lifted his head from his paws and gazed towards the front of the house. Then he uttered a loud bark.

'That will be Jonathan,' said Flavia. She pushed the glossy piles of ivy and jasmine off her lap and followed Scuto out of the garden and into the atrium.

Caudex was just opening the door. Flavia ran forward to greet her friend.

'Hello, Jonathan! Oh, hello Doctor Mordecai!' Jonathan's father entered behind his son.

'Father has something he wants to say to us.' Jonathan rolled his eyes. 'He won't tell me what it is yet . . .'

'Is Nubia here?' asked Mordecai pleasantly. He was wearing a pale blue turban and a white robe, and Flavia thought the colours made him look milder than usual.

'Yes. She's in the garden. We're making garlands.

Please come through.' She led the way into the garden and then ran to get two chairs. As she passed the open door of the kitchen she whispered, 'Alma, could you bring us some peach juice?'

'Of course, dear,' her old nurse replied. 'I'll be there in a moment.'

Flavia set the chairs by the bench and they all sat down. The three friends looked at Mordecai and he looked back with his heavy-lidded eyes. The fountain splashed and a bird repeated the same clear note high in the fig tree. Nervously, Flavia picked at a strand of ivy.

Mordecai cleared his throat.

'Miriam and Jonathan and I are very honoured to have been invited to your father's homecoming dinner this evening,' he began.

'Even though he's been home for three days now,' broke in Flavia, and then bit her lower lip.

'Yes,' smiled Mordecai. He cleared his throat again. 'However, I was sad to hear from Jonathan that you haven't invited Lupus.'

Flavia stared at Mordecai with open mouth for a moment before she remembered herself and closed it. Then she shot a glare at Jonathan. But he was gazing bleakly at Scuto, who lay panting at their feet.

'Lupus tried to steal from us!' was all she could say in her defence. 'That's why he wanted to spend the night here. He . . . he betrayed us!'

'Flavia.' Mordecai twisted a gold ring on his finger. 'And Jonathan,' he added, looking up at his son, 'do you have any idea what kind of life Lupus has led?'

'No,' admitted Flavia, hanging her head.

Jonathan just shook his miserably.

'He's been on his own in this city for as long as he can remember. He has no mother or father, as far as we know. No home, no place to be safe, no family of any kind. As if that weren't bad enough, he hasn't even got a tongue with which to communicate. You were probably the first real friends he's had in his life.'

Flavia swallowed. Her throat hurt.

'His entire life has been a fight to survive, and he must have fought very hard to have stayed alive this long. He has had to beg or steal every bite of food that's come into his poor mouth.' Mordecai sighed, and softened his tone.

'Can you not find it in your hearts to forgive him? I admit he did something that was wrong. He was tempted to steal and he gave in to that temptation. But haven't you ever given in to temptation? Haven't you ever done anything wrong?'

None of them spoke.

'Jonathan, you broke your promise to me the day you were almost kidnapped. You promised you would stay on this street. Flavia, your father told you never to go into the graveyard but you have gone there repeatedly. You know what you did was wrong, don't you?'

Flavia nodded and then blurted out, 'What about Nubia? You haven't said anything to *her.*' She immediately regretted saying such a spiteful thing and bit her lip. But Mordecai surprised her by saying,

'You're right, Flavia, I'm sure Nubia *has* done things in her life that she is ashamed of.'

Nubia raised her head and nodded. Her eyes were full of tears.

'Well,' said Mordecai gently, 'our faith teaches that if you say sorry to God for the wrong things you have done, *and* if you forgive the people who have done wrong things to you, you will be forgiven. Would you like that?'

Nubia and Jonathan nodded immediately. After a moment Flavia did, too. It sounded suspiciously easy.

'Are you sorry for all the wrong things you've done?' asked Mordecai. They all nodded this time. 'Then say sorry to God.'

'How?' asked Flavia.

'Jonathan?' said his father.

Jonathan closed his eyes and said, 'I'm sorry for all the wrong things I've done, Lord.' and then added, 'Amen.'

Straight away, Nubia closed her eyes and imitated Jonathan. 'I'm sorry for wrong things also. Amen.'

'What does "amen" mean?' Flavia asked cautiously.

'It's like saying: I really mean it,' said Mordecai with a smile.

Flavia closed her eyes and tried to imagine which god she was speaking to. Finally she settled on the beardless shepherd with a lamb over his shoulders.

'I'm sorry for all the wrong things I've done,' she whispered to him, and then added, 'amen.' When she opened her eyes a moment later she felt lighter somehow.

'And now,' said Mordecai, 'will you forgive Lupus?'

They all nodded.

'Then what are you doing sitting here? Get down to the forum and find him and invite him to your party!'

The three of them jumped up and began to run for the door.

'Wait!' said Mordecai.

They all ran back. Mordecai slipped Jonathan some coins. 'You'd better take him to the baths again.'

'Yes, father!' Jonathan grinned, and they all charged off toward the door.

'Wait!' cried Mordecai. They all ran back.

'You'd better take Caudex *and* Scuto with you this time.'

'Yes, Doctor Mordecai!' Flavia nodded vigorously, while Nubia ran to get Scuto's lead.

'Wait!' shouted Mordecai. They all ran back.

'Who's going to drink all this peach juice?' he asked, gesturing at Alma coming towards them with a tray.

'You are!' they laughed, and ran out of the garden.

It was a perfect summer evening. The warmth of the late afternoon sun had released all the scents of the garden and a sea breeze touched the leaves just enough to make them tremble. The sky was lavender and the garden was deep green, filled with cool shadows.

The nine of them were sitting or reclining in the dining room.

Miriam had been counted an adult, because at thirteen she was legally old enough to marry. Wearing a dark blue stola which set off her glossy black curls and pale skin, she reclined next to Aristo. Flavia felt a pang of jealousy. Aristo, her tutor, had sailed back from Corinth with her father. He was young and handsome with olive skin and curly hair the colour of bronze. Flavia had always imagined she would marry him when she was older.

But Miriam had been silent, as usual, and Aristo was not even looking at her. He was chatting to the merchant Cordius, who as the guest of honour reclined on the middle couch. On the third couch Mordecai reclined next to Flavia's father.

Flavia, Jonathan, Nubia and Lupus all sat round a table in the middle, so that they could be part of the conversation. All nine diners were bathed and perfumed, wearing their garlands of ivy, jasmine and grape hyacinth.

Cordius had brought along a young slave named Felix, who was helping Alma serve dinner. They had just finished the first course: bite-sized parcels of peppered goat's cheese wrapped in pickled vine leaves. Felix removed their empty plates as Alma brought in the main course, rabbit with onion and date gravy.

'This is delicious, Alma!' said Flavia's father. 'I always miss your cooking when I'm at sea.'

'I caught the rabbits this morning with my sling,' said Jonathan proudly.

'It *is* delicious,' agreed Cordius. 'Congratulations to both hunter and cook!' He lifted his wine cup.

Flavia tried not to look at Cordius. The sight of a flowered garland above his mournful face made her want to giggle. But she couldn't avoid looking at him when he said,

'I owe a great debt of gratitude to you four children.'

He made a gesture to his young slave Felix, who quietly moved to stand near the table.

'I knew there was a thief in my household. That's

why I removed the gold from my strongbox. But it was your quick action that exposed him and the crime. I know you expected no reward, but I would like to give you one.' He nodded to Felix, who handed a heavy gold coin to each of the four friends.

They all gasped. Flavia and Jonathan thanked Cordius warmly. Lupus automatically put his coin between his teeth and bit it in order to test it was really gold. His face went red as everyone laughed, but when he saw they weren't offended he smiled furtively. Nubia was staring at her reward with eyes almost as round and gold as the coin.

'You might also like to know that Avitus's widow will be looked after,' said Cordius. 'Doctor Mordecai told me about the tragic loss of her daughter and husband. She is an excellent seamstress and I have offered her a place in my household and a small allowance.'

'Very gracious of you.' Mordecai bowed his head to the merchant.

'What will you buy with your newfound riches?' Cordius asked Flavia with a rare smile.

'A complete set of Pliny's *Natural History*,' she announced without a moment's hesitation. Everyone laughed.

'Nubia?' said Captain Geminus.

'Lotus wood flute,' the girl said softly.

'Ah! We have a budding musician in the household,' Aristo leaned forward on one elbow with interest. 'I'll look forward to accompanying you on my lyre.'

'Lupus?' asked Mordecai.

Lupus shrugged. He had an odd smile on his face.

'What will you buy with *your* coin, Jonathan?' asked Flavia's father in a jolly voice, a bit too loudly.

'I'd like to buy a new watchdog,' said Jonathan. 'I've been reading Pliny's *Natural History*, too, and he writes about a kind of watchdog from India. Its mother is a dog, but its father is a tiger. It is the fiercest watchdog in the world, but they cost a fortune. I couldn't buy one before, but now perhaps I can. A watchdog that fierce would never let anyone hurt the people it protected. And nothing could hurt it either. Don't you agree, Nubia? Nubia?'

But once again, like a shadow, Nubia had disappeared.

SCROLL XXII

'How does she *do* that?' marvelled Jonathan, scratching his curly head.

'Shall we search for her?' asked Aristo from the couch.

'No,' said Flavia. 'She'll come back. She's probably just taken Scuto a bit of rabbit.'

Scuto had been shut in the storeroom as he always was when a party was given. Otherwise he would disgrace himself by begging for morsels or tripping up Alma as she came in with the soup.

'I must ask you,' said Cordius to Flavia as he took a sip of wine, 'when did you first guess the true motive for the killings?'

'Well, it was thanks to Aristo,' said Flavia shyly. Everyone looked at the young Greek tutor in surprise.

'He always tells me to use imagination as well as reason.' Flavia looked down at her plate and then back up at Cordius.

'I was lying in bed, trying to think like Aristo: if Avitus hadn't killed the dogs, then someone else must have. And if someone else killed the dogs, then what was their motive? It probably wasn't because they hated dogs!'

Everyone was listening intently, and Flavia noticed that Aristo's eyes sparkled with delight.

'Just as I was trying to imagine what motive there could be for killing dogs, Scuto barked. And I suddenly knew. It had to be the obvious motive.'

'To silence the watchdog!' cried Aristo.

'Exactly,' exclaimed Flavia. 'But why silence Jonathan's watchdog, or the watchdog across the street, or even our watchdog?'

' "If the owner of the house had known at what time of night the thief was coming, he would have kept watch and not let his house be broken into",' quoted Mordecai.

Aristo looked at him curiously. The young Greek was very well-read but did not recognise the quote.

'Yes,' Flavia was saying. 'The main reason for silencing a watchdog is to break in and steal something. But Jonathan's family doesn't have much worth stealing, and I thought we didn't either, so I concluded the target must be Cordius.'

'Logical,' murmured Aristo.

'Then, when Lupus discovered all the gold in our storeroom, I realised that *we* were the intended victims and that either Scuto would be killed, or the thief would try to frighten us away.'

'But you knew who the thief was before Lupus

told us,' said Jonathan. 'How did you work that out?'

The evening sky had darkened from violet to purple and the dog-star winked brightly above the tiled roof. Caudex came in to light the lamps and Felix cleared away the remains of the rabbit stew.

'It was simple,' Flavia ventured. 'If Libertus was telling the truth, Avitus *had* to be the killer.'

Jonathan nodded.

'If Avitus wasn't the killer, then Libertus was probably lying. And if Libertus was lying, it must have been to protect himself. Libertus said he had been drinking at the fountain. But who would drink that smelly old water when there's sweet water in your house just a few yards up the road?'

'Unless you're very thirsty!' interjected Jonathan.

'Or unless you had to wash blood off your hands or dagger! You wouldn't do *that* in front of the slaves, would you?'

'He had the head with him as we passed by,' added Jonathan. 'Probably wrapped up in his cloak. But he was standing on the other side of the fountain and we couldn't see it.'

Flavia took a sip of her watered-down wine.

'When we first went to Libertus, he gave a description which could have been almost anyone's, to throw us off the track. To make it convincing, he made up the bit about the bag, because he knew a head was missing. Later he added details which pointed to Avitus, but only after I showed him the drawing and described what Avitus had been wearing.'

'Why didn't you suspect Libertus earlier?' asked Aristo with interest.

'Well, he was so polite and handsome,' she said, reddening slightly. 'It just never occurred to me he might be bad.'

'An understandable error,' Cordius murmured, and Flavia remembered that he had been prepared to make the young freedman his son.

' "Man looks at the outward appearance, but the Lord looks at the heart",' Mordecai quoted again, and everyone nodded their agreement, though Aristo gave him another keen look.

Flavia concluded. 'As soon as I knew the culprit was Libertus, and that he probably wanted to get rid of the dogs in order to steal the treasure, I knew the real crime would soon be committed.'

'I don't understand something!' said Flavia's father in the rather loud voice he used when he'd had too much wine. 'Lupus overheard Libertus in the tavern, correct?'

'Yes,' Flavia answered.

'Then why didn't he tell you that the man he overheard was Libertus from across the street?'

'Because Lupus had never actually seen Libertus,' explained Flavia. 'Overhearing Libertus was just a piece of good luck. But if Lupus hadn't told us, or were so long that they had to be divided into several scrolls. Pliny's *Natural History* was 37 scrolls long!

sesterces (sess-*tur*-seez)

a large brass coin worth about a day's wages

stola (*stole*-a)

a girl's or woman's dress

stylus (*stile*-us)

a metal, wood or ivory tool for writing on wax tablets

toga virilis (*toe*-ga *veer*-ill-us)

pure white toga worn by boys after 16th birthday

Torah (*tor*-ah)

The Hebrew scriptures, can refer to the first five books of the Old Testament or the entire Old Testament

tunic (*tiu*-nick)

a piece of clothing like a big T-shirt. Boys and girls usually wore a long-sleeved one

Venalicius (ven-a-*lee*-kee-us)

A Roman name; means 'slave-dealer' in Latin

Vespasian (vess-*pay*-zhun)

Roman Emperor during the time of this story (ruled 69–79)

Virgil (*vur*-jill)

A famous Latin poet who died about 60 years before this story takes place; he wrote the *Aeneid*

wax tablet

a wax-covered rectangle of wood; when the wax was scraped away, the wood beneath showed as a mark.

impluvium (im-*ploo*-vee-um)

a rainwater pool under a skylight in the atrium

Mordecai (*mord*-ak-eye)

a Hebrew name

necropolis (neck-*rop*-o-liss)

'city of the dead', graveyard outside the city walls

papyrus (pa-*pie*-rus)

the cheapest writing material, made of Egyptian reeds

pater (*pa*-ter)

the Latin word for 'father'

patrician (pa-*trish*-un)

a person from the upper classes of Rome

peristyle (*pair*-i-stile)

a row of columns around garden or courtyard

Roman numerals

the Romans used capital letters to stand for numbers. Here are a few Roman numerals and their equivalents.

I = 1	VI = 6	XI = 11	XVI = 16
II = 2	VII = 7	XII = 12	XVII = 17
III = 3	VIII = 8	XIII = 13	XVIII = 18
IV = 4	IX = 9	XIV = 14	XIX = 19
V = 5	X = 10	XV = 15	XX = 20
L = 50	C = 100	D = 500	M = 1000

scroll (skrole)

a papyrus or parchment 'book', unrolled from side to side, (not top to bottom), as it was read. Some books

They all burst out laughing and Felix came round with the wine again.

'I'm afraid we must go soon,' said Mordecai apologetically, and winced as he waited for his children to protest.

But they were too busy cooing over Tigris, who was licking rabbit gravy off Jonathan's finger.

'Before you go,' said Captain Geminus to Mordecai, 'I have a proposal for you. I must be off again soon, making the most of the sailing season. After all that's happened this past month I would like to send Flavia and Nubia somewhere safer.

'My brother has a large villa south of here on the bay of Neapolis, and he says he would be delighted to receive a houseful of people for the month of August. Your children are both invited, and you are very welcome, too.'

'Would we be able to take the puppies with us?' asked Miriam, looking up from Tigris.

'Of course!' said Flavia's father. 'Scuto will be going, though Alma and Caudex will remain here to keep an eye on things. I think they deserve a rest, too.'

'Oh please, can we go father?' begged Miriam and Jonathan.

'I'll think about it,' said Mordecai, with a smile.

Captain Geminus turned to Lupus, who was stroking Nipur and keeping his head down.

'Lupus, we would be honoured if you would come, too.'

Flavia, Nubia and Jonathan cheered and urged Lupus to come.

Lupus looked up at them and nodded once, gruffly. Then he lowered his head again and examined Nipur's tail with intense concentration.

'Of course,' added Captain Geminus, 'Aristo will be accompanying you, so there will be lessons in Greek, philosophy, art and music every morning . . .'

They all moaned.

'Then we shall definitely come!' announced Mordecai.

They all cheered.

'To a peaceful August in Pompeii, then,' said Flavia's father, and raised his cup in a toast.

'Pompeii,' they all echoed, and raised their wine cups.

FINIS

ARISTO'S SCROLL

Aeneas (a-*nee*- ass)
   Trojan son of the goddess Venus who escaped from
   conquered Troy to have many adventures and finally
   settle in what would become Rome
Aeneid (a-*nee*- id)
   long poem by the famous poet Virgil about the
   Roman hero Aeneas
amphora (am-*for*-a)
   large clay storage jar for holding wine, oil or grain
atrium (*eh*-tree-um)
   the reception room in larger Roman homes, often
   with skylight and rainwater pool
brazier (bray-zher)
   coal-filled metal bowl on legs used to heat a room
   (like an ancient radiator)
bulla (*bull*-a)
   amulet of leather or metal worn by freeborn children
carruca (ca-*ru*-ka)
   a four-wheeled travelling coach, often covered
centaur (*sen*-tawr)
   mythological creature: half man, half horse

centurion (sent-*yur*-ee-on)
> soldier in the Roman army in charge of at least a
> hundred men

ceramic (sir-*am*-ik)
> clay which has been fired in a kiln, very hard and
> smooth.

Cerberus (*sur*-bur-uss)
> the mythical three-headed dog who guarded the gates
> of hell

cicada (sick-*eh*-dah)
> an insect like a grasshopper that chirrs during the
> day

Claudius (*clawd*-ee-uss)
> Roman Emperor (ruled 41–54 AD) who built the new
> harbour two miles north of Ostia

colonnade (coll-a-*nade*)
> a covered walkway lined with columns

finis (*fin*-iss)
> Latin for 'the end'

Flavia (*flay*-vee-a)
> a girl's name, meaning 'fair-haired'

forum (*for*-um)
> ancient marketplace and civic centre in Roman
> towns

freedman (*freed*-man)
> a slave who has been granted freedom

fresco (*fress*-ko)
> painting done on the plaster of a wall when still wet:
> when plaster dries the painting is part of the wall

'They're wonderful!' said Jonathan in an odd, choked voice. 'Was the father . . .?'

Nubia looked at him and nodded. The puppies looked like miniature versions of the fierce black hound who had first led the feral pack.

'What will you do with them, Nubia?' laughed Captain Geminus.

Nubia held one up and hugged it.

'I keep it?' she asked.

'Of course!' Flavia and her father answered together.

Nubia, her head bent, hugged the puppy as tightly as she dared. After a moment she looked up, with tears sparkling on her eyelashes and said, 'I name him Nipur. Name of my dog at home.'

'Nipur it is then,' said Captain Geminus, in a hearty, booming voice, and wiped something out of his own eye.

'And the other one,' said Jonathan quietly. 'What will you name him?'

'I don't name him. You name him,' said Nubia, handing the other puppy to Jonathan. 'Don't get tiger dog.'

Jonathan took the small, squeaking bundle carefully, almost reverently, and kissed its wet black nose.

'I will name him Tigris,' said Jonathan solemnly, 'and he will be my tiger dog. Oh, Pollux! He's just peed on me!'

shown us what he looked like, we might never have solved the crime.'

Cordius toasted Lupus and the rest followed suit.

At that moment Alma came in with their dessert course. She held a tray of hot pastry cases filled with honey and walnuts, each of them in the shape of a little dog.

Everyone made noises of great approval and appreciation. They each took one, and sucked the honey off their scalded fingers.

Bright stars pricked a sky which was not yet quite black, but deepest blue. The sweet fragrance of the jasmine and hyacinth garlands filled the air.

Suddenly Nubia stepped into the soft golden lamplight of the dining room.

'Nubia!' they all greeted her.

'Have a honey and walnut dog!'

'Have a drop more wine.'

'Where have you been?'

'Graveyard,' said Nubia and crouched in the centre of the dining room. Carefully, she placed her woollen cloak on the marble floor. In its folds squirmed two small creatures.

'Oh!' breathed Miriam, jumping down from her couch. 'They're adorable!'

Everyone leaned forward to see the two little puppies, only a few weeks old, which lay squeaking on Nubia's cloak.

THE LAST SCROLL

Ostia, the port of ancient Rome, was and is a real place.

Today, it is one of the nicest ancient sites in the Mediterranean. Located about sixteen miles outside Rome, Ostia Antica (ancient Ostia) is not to be confused with the modern town of Ostia Lido (Ostia beach).

If you visit the site of Ostia Antica, you can see the remains of many warehouses, inns, temples, public baths and houses.

Some places in this story are real: the theatre and synagogue, for example. Other places are made up, like Flavia's house and Aurarius's workshop. But they *could* be there, we just haven't found them.

CAROLINE LAWRENCE

Caroline Lawrence is American. She grew up in California and came to England when she won a scholarship to Cambridge to study Classical Archaeology. She lives by the river in London with her husband, a writer and graphic designer. In 2009, Caroline was awarded the Classics Association Prize for 'a significant contribution to the public understanding of Classics'.

She also writes *The Roman Mystery Scrolls* – a hilarious and action-packed series of shorter mysteries featuring Threptus, a former beggar boy turned apprentice to a Roman soothsayer.

And don't miss Caroline's whip-cracking new series, *The P.K. Pinkerton Mysteries*, set in America's Wild West and starring Virginia City's newest detective, P.K. Pinkerton, as he fights crime against a backdrop of gamblers, gunslingers and deadly desperados!

Choose one of the twin portals on Caroline's website www.carolinelawrence.com to enter
Ancient Rome www.romanmysteries.com
The Wild West www.pkpinkerton.com